ALLIANCE

due SOUTH™

due SOUTH™

Produced, written and compiled by Michael Mouland

KEY PORTER BOOKS

Canadian Cataloguing in Publication Data

Due south: the official guide

ISBN 1-55013-966-5

1. Due south (Television program).

PN1992.77.D83D83 1998   791.45'72   C98-931422-7

THE CANADA COUNCIL | LE CONSEIL DES ARTS
FOR THE ARTS | DU CANADA
SINCE 1957 | DEPUIS 1957

The publisher gratefully acknowledges the support of the Canada Council for the Arts and the Ontario Arts Council for its publishing program.

Key Porter Books Limited
70 The Esplanade
Toronto, Ontario
Canada M5E 1R2

www.keyporter.com

Design: Lightfoot Art & Design Inc.

Distributed in the United States by Firefly Books

Printed and bound in Canada

98 99 00 01 6 5 4 3 2 1

Contents

You're under arrest! Members of the musical ride get their man. ("All The Queen's Horses")

About the Author

Sir John A. Macdonald

was Canada's first prime minister and minister of justice. He conceived of and formed the Royal Canadian Mounted Police after being inspired by the "mounted rifle" units of the United States Army working in the early American West, as well as the Royal Irish Constabulary. The RCMP (initially called the North-West Mounted Police) was formed by Act of Parliament on May 23, 1873, to bring justice to the North-West Territories (at that time including present-day Alberta and Saskatchewan). Between 1874 to 1905 the RCMP established amicable relations with Native peoples, and to this day it serves as a peacekeeping force in Canada's remote and more populated areas.

I pretty much left the boy to his own devices when he was growing up.

Some would say that I was perhaps a bit neglectful by being away so much, but I can see that Benton didn't suffer too much from his upbringing. I know he's not bitter or resentful about my long absences, and our relationship, such as it was, didn't diminish Benton's feelings towards me. After all, the reason the boy has ended up in Chicago was because of me; he wanted to track down my murderers, not to put too fine a point on things. Had he not cared about the fact that I expired prematurely at 57 as a result of my investigation into the cause of caribou drownings a number of years ago, Benton would still be fighting crime in the Territories. His soft spot for my cabin is a testament to his love of the North, and his sojourns there are solid evidence of his continued affection for me, I'm certain.

Introduction by

Benton keeps some rough company in Chicago, and his chum Ray could do with a little polishing sometimes. Not that I'm one to pass judgment on the company the boy keeps, and I have to remind myself that each of us has a responsibility to ourselves to lead our lives the way we see fit. But when Benton is looking for advice, I hope that he always feels free to knock on my door, however long it remains open. From where I stand—that is, with two feet very much in the grave—I can only make up for lost time during the boy's childhood by serving as a sort of consultant in his current life. I'm not keen on imposing my views on the boy, but I feel that he requires my years of experience from time to time, even when he doesn't specifically ask for it. In fact I'm certain that he can benefit from my take on situations and from my moral outlook. If the truth be told, *(deceased)* I hate being an old monkey on the boy's shoulder. But to leave him without kin in a big, bad American city would be taking my philosophy of leaving the boy to fend for himself a little too far. So, from the afterlife, I intervene in young Benton's life when there is a need. Frobisher understands my position, I hope.

Benton has had little experience when it comes to the wiles of the fairer sex, and I regret that I wasn't around to dissuade the boy from entering into that rather unpleasant episode with Victoria—what the Americans would call "a bad date." The wiles of a bad woman can be hard to resist, I know. It is against my principles to advise the boy in matters of the heart, though I do see him bedding down with Mademoiselle Thatcher; and, truthfully, I've done a little to encourage the boy to indulge in the delicacies that life sometimes presents. Benton's mother, God bless her soul, knew of where I stood in this regard, and the boy is the fruit of our labors, if one must think of it as work. And I don't apologize for the fact that Benton was born in a barn, which I assume helped the boy take life by the horns, as it were, and helped with his sense of self-sufficiency.

Scrapbook

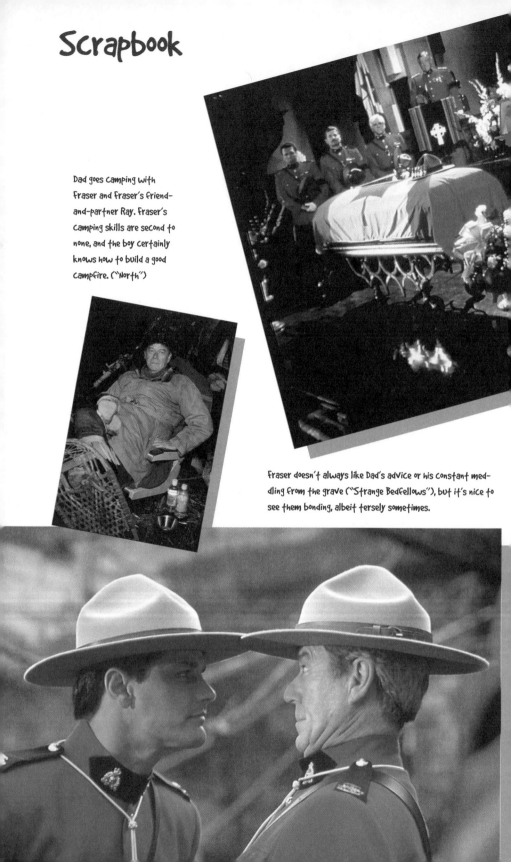

Dad goes camping with Fraser and Fraser's friend-and-partner Ray. Fraser's camping skills are second to none, and the boy certainly knows how to build a good campfire. ("North")

Fraser doesn't always like Dad's advice or his constant meddling from the grave ("Strange Bedfellows"), but it's nice to see them bonding, albeit tersely sometimes.

Time to meet the Maker: funerals are so depress-ing, especially when they're your own. Frobisher and Benton wouldn't see the last of the likes of me, much to their dismay. ("The Pilot")

Reality Check

Gordon Pinsent

Gordon Pinsent is virtually syn-onymous with Canadian film, television and theater, and has been recognized for his accom-plishments by being bestowed with the Order of Canada. His thirty-year career has been diverse, to say the least, with appearances on *Hogan's Heroes*, *Cannon* and *Marcus Welby, M.D.* He has won two Gemini Awards for best actor, produced four plays and performed in more than eighty professional productions. He currently hosts the CBC program *Life and Times*.

Some of Dad's Sage Advice to Benton

fraser:

You always told me that the most important thing a man can do is his duty. I'm about to embark on a somewhat devious course of action, and I'm not entirely sure where my duty actually lies.

robert fraser:

Nineteen sixty-one. I was ordered to help 32 Inuit families relocate 500 miles further north on Ellesmere Island. We had some dispute with the Russians—this was long before the Canada Cup. We wanted to demonstrate our sovereignty over the Far North. Now, I'd been up to Ellesmere and I knew that life there would be hard if not impossible. I said as much to my superiors, but they were adamant. And I had my orders.

fraser:

So what did you do?

robert fraser:

The only thing I could do. I went up to Ellesmere, marked out 32 plots of land, threw up a flag, opened up a post office. Tom Goforth, a young man from one of the families, lived up there all alone for the first year. He collected all the relocation checks and forwarded them back to the families, who used the money to hire a lawyer. He won the case against their relocation in court.

fraser:

So you created a fictitious town?

robert fraser:

Ellesmere was listed in Maclean's *that year as having the lowest crime rate in North America. Your heart is where your duty lies, son. Your head is just along to help with the driving.*

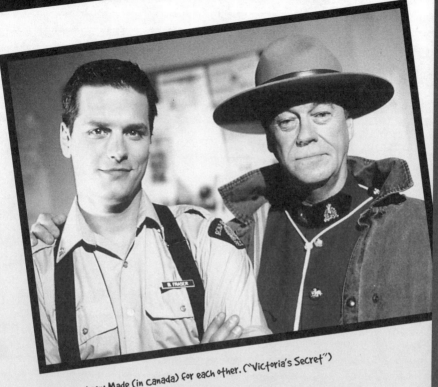

Father and son: Made (in Canada) for each other. ("Victoria's Secret")

Sgt. Robert Fraser

- height: 5 feet 8 inches (173 cm)
- died at age 57 when he was murdered by an assassin
- a career officer with the RCMP, spent 35 years with the force
- Sgt. Robert Fraser's wife, Caroline, died young, when Benton was six years old; Benton was turned over to his grandparents for his upbringing
- had two good friends: Buck Frobisher and Gerard, who is now likely in Robert's bad books because he is the "friend" who had Robert murdered

Fraser and Fraser Sr. have been known to cook up a good plan of action from time to time ("The Gift of the Wheelman"), but they do have their disagreements.

Fraser's arrival in the Windy City

was not without some consternation on his part, though he would never admit as much. Possessing only a modicum of experience with city life and what it offers (or doesn't, depending on your point of view), Fraser hit the streets running—or, er, walking, because his politeness preceded him when he kept giving up his cabs to others waiting in line at O'Hare Airport. The nation's third largest city, Chicago covers more than 227 square miles (588 km²) and stretches some 33 miles (53 km) along Lake Michigan. Chicago boasts a population of 3 million, living in 76 neighborhoods. A far cry indeed from the sparsely populated reaches of Fraser's northern Canadian homeland, until you consider that Chicago's history is deeply rooted in a Native past, just like Fraser's. Chicago gets its name from the Illini Indian word for "wild onion" or "strong and

great," Che-cau-gou. Early European explorers came to this part of the New World as fur trappers; so that Fraser's stomping grounds were originally the domain of the Hudson's Bay Company, fur trappers and traders extraordinaire. But fur, dead animals (remember those drowned caribou) and Indians aren't the only recurring themes in Fraser's life. Chicago is also known for its pizza (think Ray Vecchio),its criminal past (think Al Capone) and its cold winters (think Northwest Territories). In fact, Chicago has all the things necessary to be a fitting place for a Mountie. The Windy City even has a Canadian consulate. Who could ask for anything more?

Chicago's nickname, the "Windy City," has nothing to do with the weather, though some would have you believe it. The city's nickname has more to do with the wind expelled by the city's first politicians. Political life here has always been hot, hot, hot, and the grandstanding, debating and intrigue that traditionally go along with any political activity were raised to a high art.

lt. welsh:
You see, sir, Constable Fraser doesn't lie.

cahill:
That's an admirable quality in times of peace, but we are in the middle of a war, a war against crime and corruption, and I demand your cooperation. The city of Chicago demands your cooperation.

fraser:
And you shall have it, sir. To the full extent of the law.

cahill:
Are you mocking me? Are you mocking this city, this administration?

fraser:
Certainly not, sir. No. We greatly appreciate the generosity shown to us by the people of Chicago. And I assure you, should you ever find yourself in Nunavut, you will not be wanting for a meal.

cahill:
You know this Marquess of Queensberry thing and your grammar and all? It's very quaint, but I just want to remind you that we took Grenada, we beat the snot out of Haiti, we knocked Panama on its ass and if needs be, we can take this little pisspot too. Have a nice evening.

The Chicago PD

The Chicago PD's 27th precinct, headed by Lt. Harding Welsh, is a far different operation than the department's checkered history—all linked to the city's notorious mob past—would suggest. Crime, corruption and greed were the ruling principles between 1920 and 1933, when the mob battled for control over bootlegging and other lucrative, illegal vice activities that resulted in more than 700 murders during the city's famous gangland years. The Chicago PD was knee-deep in the filth of crime and corruption festering in the city's underbelly.

     Precinct captain and brothel operator Big Jim Colosimo built a small crime empire and ended up controlling the South Side's liquor and illegal gaming operations. In true gangland style, Capt. Colosimo caught a bullet in the head outside a restaurant he owned. Al Capone was among the 5000 attendees at Colosimo's funeral, which also attracted prominent judges and politicians. Colosimo's successor continued to keep the police force in his back pocket with bribes and payoffs, and Al Capone eventually came to control the territory once ruled by Colosimo.

     More than 50 years later Chicago still can't seem to shake its notorious past. Internal investigations by Damon Cahill and his people are endured by Lt. Welsh, who has gone out on a limb to protect Ray Vecchio from the State Attorney's Office aspirant while Vecchio stays deep undercover.

CONVENTIONS & TOURISM

Conventions, trade shows, corporate meetings (annual)	30,082
Attendance	3,420,584
Expenditures	$2,681,828,758
Pleasure visitors (estimate)	11,600,000

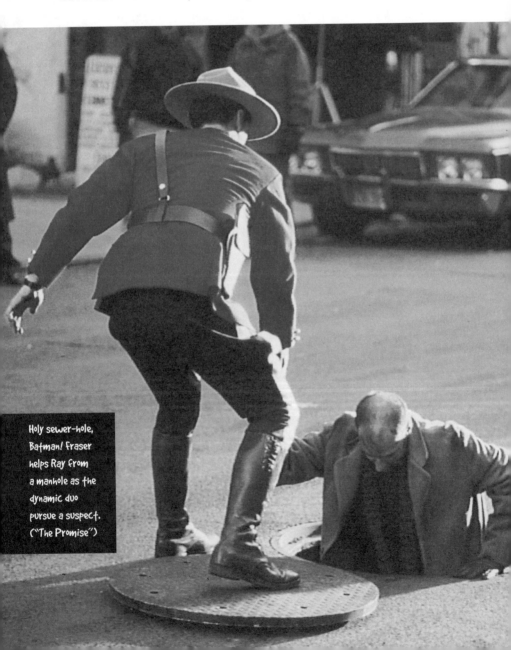

Holy sewer-hole, Batman! Fraser helps Ray from a manhole as the dynamic duo pursue a suspect. ("The Promise")

POPULATION

GROSS POPULATION	3,783,726
Caucasian	1,263,524
African American	1,087,711
Asian	104,118
Native American	7,064
Other Races	321,309

TALLEST BUILDINGS (1990)

Sears Tower	110 stories	1,454 feet	(443 m)
AMOCO Building	80 stories	1,136 feet	(346 m)
John Hancock Center	100 stories	1,127 feet	(344 m)
311 S. Wacker Drive	65 stories	970 feet	(296 m)
Two Prudential Plaza	64 stories	912 feet	(278 m)

WATER

Daily average pumpage (gallons)	1,066,000,000 (4,846,000,000 litres)
Annual pumpage (gallons)	390,156,000,000 (1,773,649,000,000 litres)
Total current connections (metered & assessed)	492,245

SEWERS

Sewers mains (approx.)	4,352 miles (7002 km)
Catch basins (estimate)	213,000
Manholes (estimate)	148,000

SOURCE: Chicago Information System 1998

"Spy vs. Spy"

An ode to the *Mad* magazine comic strip of the same name, this action-packed episode pits Fraser against two gun-smuggling operatives spun off from the defunct KGB. Fraser and Kowalski team up with Albert Hanrahan, an old man who believes he is a spy and receives radio signals through a metal plate in his head. Albert is attacked and in the ensuing scuffle to apprehend the assailant, Kowalski kills the suspect. Fraser later determines at the morgue that Hanrahan's attacker killed himself by biting down on a cyanide-capped molar, which leads Fraser to deduce that the old man's role in this turn of events is somehow linked. Fraser and Diefenbaker track Hanrahan to his girlfriend's apartment and discover a clue: a ballet ticket.

Fraser suits up in his best duds and takes his seat at the ballet next to a woman with an eastern-European accent who speaks in ciphers. When Fraser is accosted by the mysterious woman's armed sidekicks he takes to the stage to escape. The auditorium of ballet-goers are at first aghast but the mountie does some fancy footwork with the dancers on stage before escaping on a flying horse that lifts him off the stage to safety. Fraser escapes out a back door and jumps into a black limousine that happens to be waiting there for him. Driven by Pike, a secret agent who works for a government organization that is so secret that even he doesn't know what it does, Fraser gets a bit of a rundown on what he's become involved in. Pike drops Fraser off and uses Kowalski's apartment as a safe house for Hanrahan and his girlfriend Ruth while the two policemen investigate what turns out to be a case revolving around Russian arms dealing and a mysterious spy who goes by the name of "Nautilus."

"It just takes a few extra seconds to be courteous." That's a motto I like to live by.

I first came to Chicago on the trail of my father's killers, and for reasons that don't need explaining at this juncture I've remained attached as liaison by the Canadian consulate. I'm in Chicago in a strictly unofficial capacity.

Those who don't know me might assume that I miss my father greatly, and I do. But I'm blessed with the presence of his apparition from time to time, when he drops in to offer advice. Others might say he meddles in my life since he doesn't have one of his own any more. But I see it differently, and take his appearances as demonstrations of affection for a son he seldom saw growing up.

Since moving to Chicago with Dief I've found a good friend in Ray. I admit he's a bit ragged around the edges sometimes, but I have to remind myself that I'm a stranger in a strange land and he has a good heart.

And a strange land it is sometimes. I won't pass judgment except to say that the residents of Chicago try to be upstanding citizens even in the face of the law-breaking that goes on here. God knows I try to help Ray and Lt. Welsh out when I can, and Dief doesn't seem to mind (though who knows what Dief thinks?). Our joint effort to combat the criminal element is a labor of love mostly, but I think the Chicago PD really needs the help because of understaffing. Elaine understands, and I certainly prefer fighting crime in my spare time to watching TV, though maybe I'd get more out of it if I fixed the sound on the set that one of my generous neighbors lent me. This is a country that really enjoys television, that's for sure.

I've learned to speak American English and to pronounce things differently. Like schedule, where the "c" is hard and stands in for the "sh" sound of our Canadian version. (Words like schedule are spelled the same, though.) But tell me why lieutenant is pronounced "lootenant" instead of the correct "leftenant"? I'm hoping to gain a better command of the American language, but in the meantime I'll bumble through using my own version of the Queen's English.

I'm finding that there is no limit to good etiquette, even in the face of the hustle and bustle of city life. The importance of treating others with respect is among the things I learned as a boy from the Inuit, who taught me a thing or two growing up in the Territories. Granted, I did learn a lot from the books lent to me by my grandparents, who operated

Reality check
PaulGross

Const. Benton Fraser is played by actor Paul Gross. Besides acting in and producing *Due South*, Gross is an accomplished playwright, with stints as a writer-in-residence at the Stratford Festival and the National Arts Centre in Ottawa. He has also written episodes for a variety of television productions and has been nominated for numerous Gemini Awards. His other screen appearances include *Chasing Rainbows*, *Getting Married in Buffalo Jump*, *Cold Comfort*, *Aspen Extreme* and *Tales of the City*. Being the son of a career soldier meant that his youth was filled with travel. He was born in Calgary, Alberta, and attended schools in England, Washington, D.C., and Canada. He graduated from the University of Alberta in Edmonton with a degree in drama.

Another insane moment for Fraser and Ray, all in the name of justice. ("Hawk and Handsaw")

a library in China before the Revolution and later moved it to the Territories, where I was given borrowing privileges.

Ray thinks I'm living in my own snow globe. And the new Ray—well, we won't go into that—has referred to me as a "freak." I guess that goes with the territory.

Thank you kindly.

25

Fraser and Ray have some interesting
assignments: as Bertie and Jeeves in
"The Edge".

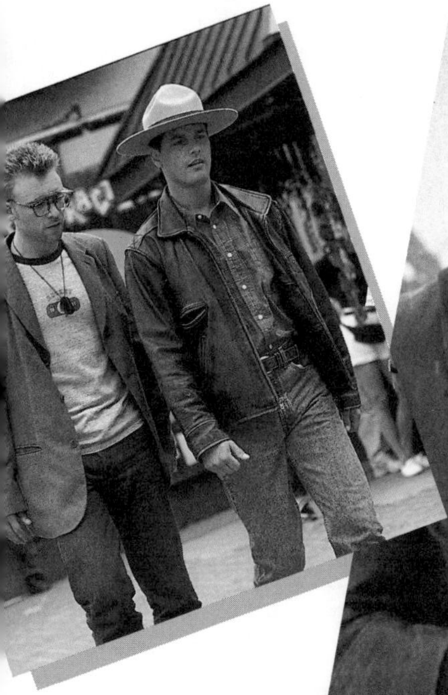

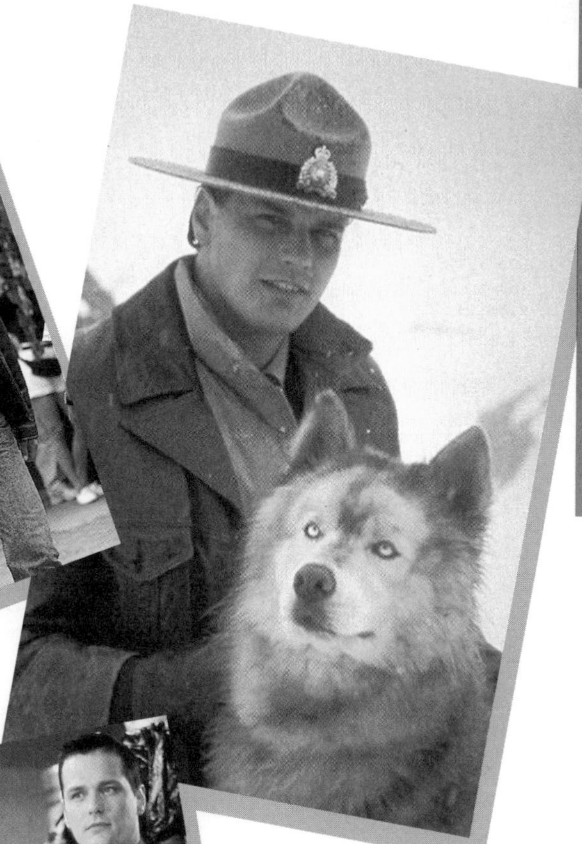

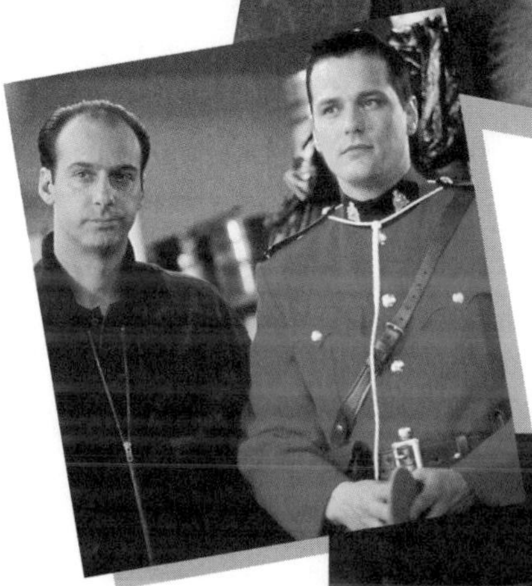

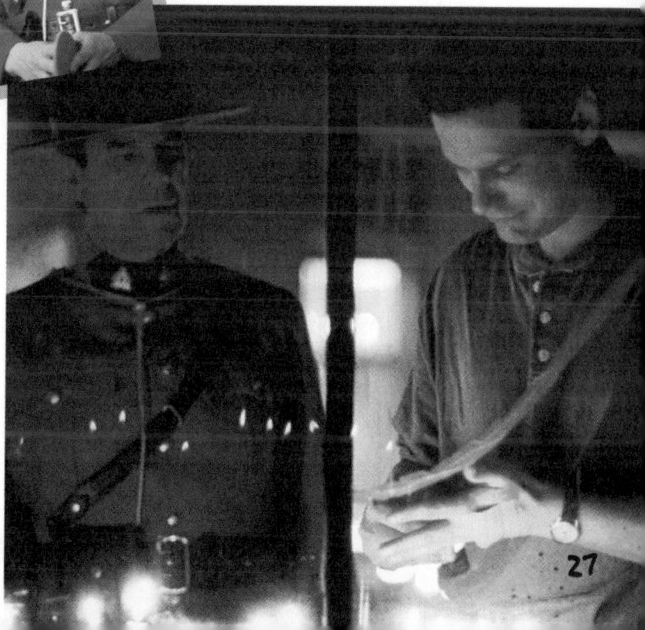

- makes his home at the Canadian consulate in Chicago. His apartment at 15 W. Racine, #3J, Chicago, IL, burned down.

- about 35 years old, a career Mountie with more than 15 years' experience on the force

- Fraser's love life is sparse, to say the least. Victoria Metcalfe was Fraser's only true love, but he put her in prison for robbing a bank. He has also had flirtatious dalliances with other women, including his boss, Inspector Meg Thatcher, and a bounty hunter named Janet Morse. Fraser seems almost oblivious to the advances of Ray's sister, Francesca, and legions of other women.

- Because his father, Robert Fraser, was away from home so much, Fraser was raised mostly by his grandparents, who were librarians living in Inuvik, Tuktoyaktuk and Alert.

- speaks French, English, Chinese (Cantonese and Mandarin) and Inuktitut (a less complex language that is easier than English for Dief to understand); understands Greek and Latin; can sign in semaphore

- types at 100 words per minute and demonstrates advanced computer skills

- has an extraordinary sense of smell and taste, and is known for his superior tracking skills (taught to him by the Inuit); has been known to taste the dirt on the bottom of shoes and is able to track Dief by following a trail of the canine's piddle

- favorite poets include Robert Service and Gerard Manley Hopkins

- does not lie

- friends include Ray Vecchio, Diefenbaker, Sgt. Duncan Buck Frobisher and Mark Smithbauer, a hockey player whom Fraser doesn't keep in touch with much. He fondly remembers a childhood friend named Innusiq

- wears one of two red serge uniforms to work, as well as a brown uniform and "civvies" (blue jeans), all worn with his signature Mountie Stetson

- Fraser's Uncle Tiberius died "wrapped in cabbage leaves" in "a freak accident" according to Fraser's father, who refused to get more specific.

- a distant relative (a fourth cousin, once removed) by the name of Malaka Unyear had his ear up to a shell and was listening to the gentle sound of the surf when a narwhal poked through the nearby ice and shoved the seashell into his eardrum. The gentle lapping of the surf, from that day onward, became instead a rushing torrent raging through his cranium

- retires to his father's cabin for vacations in "the Territories"

- is pretty handy with a knife, being able to throw one like an expert dart thrower; attributes his expert "knifemanship" to the "five Ps": Proper Preparation Prevents Poor Performance

Bang! There goes the cottage! ("The Pilot")

A little Hamburger Helper for these pigs in a blanket. Sheathed in blankets made of meat, Fraser and Ray brave out a long, cold night in a meat locker. ("They Eat Horses, Don't They?")

I love a man in a uniform: Francesca hangs on to every one of Benton's words, even in church during choir practice, where all libidinous thoughts are supposedly banished. ("The Deal")

Top 10 Episodes

"Red, White or Blue"

Patriotism knows no limits in this powder keg of an episode that sees Fraser and Vecchio strapped to a bomb at the trial of terrorist Randall Bolt who was the leader in the failed attempt to kidnap a trainload of mounties in "All the Queen's Horses." Ray is jealous of the fact that Fraser is the star witness in Bolt's trial but soon realizes that the extra attention isn't worth it when he and Fraser are attached to a bomb that is set to go off when the two crime fighters' combined heart rate reaches 200 beats per minute.

Randall Bolt's family also takes the entire courtroom hostage, along with the judge and jury, and the criminals make a demand for a helicopter that will fly them away. The already-tense situation heightens as Fraser tries to calm Ray while trying at the same time to defuse the bomb.

*L*aw enforcement is a dangerous game, and Fraser's run-ins with the criminal element have resulted in temporary paralysis, temporary blindness, cuts and bruises from being beaten up, amnesia, and unconsciousness from blows to the head (three times, no less, when Dief tried to rescue him from a mine shaft that had been converted to a bear trap by poachers).

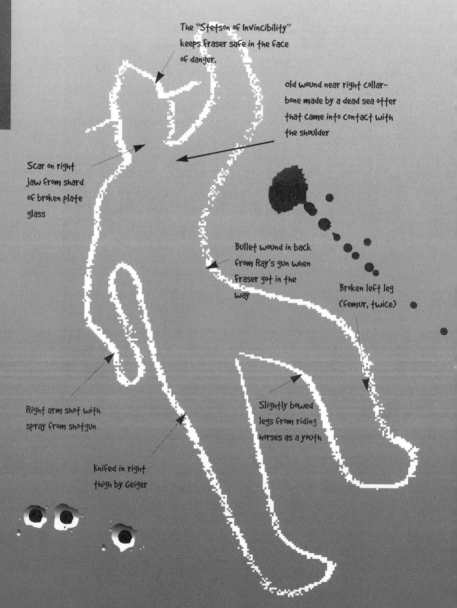

The "Stetson of Invincibility" keeps Fraser safe in the face of danger.

old wound near right collarbone made by a dead sea otter that came into contact with the shoulder

Scar on right jaw from shard of broken plate glass

Bullet wound in back from Ray's gun when Fraser got in the way

Broken left leg (femur, twice)

Right arm shot with spray from shotgun

Slightly bowed legs from riding horses as a youth

Knifed in right thigh by Geiger

Magical Things in *Due South*

• **The Stetson of Invincibility:** Fraser seemingly runs into trouble when he and his hat became detached.

• **The Dream Catcher:** A birthday present to Ray Kowalski from Fraser; Ray used the Native token to locate the source of his childhood anxieties.

• **The Apparitions:** Ray Vecchio's father and Fraser's father have made appearances to counsel their respective sons on various matters. Fraser's father carries on a ghostly operation from an office in Fraser's closet at the consulate, appearing at moments of distress in Fraser's life. Only Fraser and Buck Frobisher have the ability to see and converse with the apparition.

• **Hypnotism:** Another of Fraser's less conventional skills was used in the pursuit of justice when he hypnotized the witnesses to a murder. Ray was skeptical, calling the method "mumbo jumbo voodoo jujitsu hocus pocus," but, as usual, Fraser got his man.

The Windhover
(To Christ Our Lord)

I caught this morning morning's minion, king-
dom of daylight's dauphin, dapple-dawn-drawn Falcon, in his riding
Of the rolling level underneath him steady air, and striding
High there, how he rung upon the rein of a wimpling wing

In his ecstasy! then off, off forth on swing,
As a skate's heel sweeps smooth on a bow-bend: the hurl and gliding
Rebuffed the big wind. My heart in hiding
Stirred for a bird,-the achieve of, the mastery of the thing!

Brute beauty and valour and act, oh, air, pride, plume, here
Buckle! AND the fire that breaks from thee then, a billion
Times told lovelier, more dangerous, O my chevalier!
No wonder of it: sheer plod makes plough down sillion
Shine, and blue-bleak embers, ah my dear,
Fall, gall themselves, and gash gold-vermilion.

Gerard Manley Hopkins
(1845 – 1889)

The World of the Inuit
Fraser's Formative Years

The influence of the Inuit in Fraser's life cannot be overestimated. Not only did Fraser learn Inuktitut from the people of the North—commonly referred to as "Eskimos"—but he also learned his remarkable tracking skills from the Inuit (which means "the people" in their language). It is no wonder that these people influenced Fraser's life, for there are some 56,000 Inuit living in 53 communities across the North.

The Inuit culture is deeply rooted in the land and its cycles, and as such it is a necessity for these people to interpret the complexities of wildlife and the environment in their quest for survival. Traditionally, the Inuit did not believe that their status as humans gave them precedence over the environment or other animals. The Inuit therefore afforded no more respect to themselves than to the animals that shared their harsh environment. Sharing and cooperation—two principles inherited by Fraser in his day-to-day dealings with people—are key to Inuit society. Everyone does his or her part to help those in need; food is shared and provided to those who are in need. The diet consists mainly of marine mammals, and animal skins are typically used as clothing: caribou skins for parkas sealskin for boots, animal fur for the lining of parka hoods.

The Inuit inhabit the Northwest Territories, as well as regions in Labrador and northern Quebec. Historically, they have lived in the area bordered by the Mackenzie Delta in the west, the Labrador coast in the east, the southern point of Hudson Bay in the south, and the High Arctic islands in the north. With such snowy regions as their stomping grounds, they are adept at coping with an ice-coated environment and traverse the frozen tundra via dogsled.

To catch a thief: A thief inside the Natural History Museum suspends himself over a case containing ancient Tsimshian stone masks. ("The Mask")

Inuktitut means "to sound like an Inuk." True northerners, Fraser speaks fluent Inuktitut and Diefenbaker can lip-read the language. Although Inuktitut has been spoken for thousands of years, the language has only been put into writing in recent years. History and legend were traditionally passed down orally. A syllabic script developed for the Cree language was adapted for the eastern Arctic and looks like this:

a	◁	u	▷	i	△		ᵇ
pa	<	pu	>	pi	Λ	p	<
ta	⊂	tu	⊃	ti	∩	t	⊂
ka	ᵇ	ku	ᵈ	ki	ρ	k	ᵇ
ga	ᶫ	gu	J	gi	⌐	g	ᶫ
ma	⌐	mu	⌐	mi	⌐	m	⌐
na	ᵃ	nu	ᵇ	ni	σ	n	ᵃ
sa	˥	su	⌐	si	⌐	s	˥
la	⊂	lu	⊃	li	⌐	l	⊂
ja	˥	ju	⌐	ji	⌐	j	˥
va	≪	vu	ᵖ	vi	Λ	v	≪
ra	ˢ	ru	?	ri	⌐	r	ˢ
qa	ᵖ	qu	ᵈ	qi	ᵖ	q	ᵈ
nga	ˢᶫ	ngu	ˢJ	ngi	ˢ⌐	ng	ˢᶫ
&a	⌐	&u	⌐	&i	⌐	&	⌐

FRASER: According to the textbooks, a wolf is a hunter, an animal of prey. The Inuit take a very different view of it. The people of the North. They have their own idea of why the wolf was created:

In the beginning, so goes the legend, there was a man and woman, and nothing else on the earth walked or swam or flew. And so the woman dug a big hole in the ground and she started fishing in it. She pulled out all the animals. The last was the caribou. And so the woman set the caribou free and ordered it to multiply, and soon the land was full of them. The people lived well and were happy. But the hunters, the hunters only killed those caribou that were big and strong, and soon all that was left were the weak and the sick. And the people realized that the caribou and the wolf were one. For although the caribou feeds the wolf, it is the wolf that keeps the caribou strong.

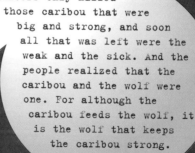

A Trojan train: Mounties on horseback emerge from...   the bowels of a train, charge over a hilltop, and surround

Ride Forever

I was born north of Great Slave, 1898
And I rode near all my life on a ranch
near Devil's Gate
And I've seen this world about me
bend and flip and change
Hey, it feels like rain—that's a thun-
der cloud
Well, I've been called a coward but
I've seen two world wars
And I lost my son Virgil, my Korean
reward
And my Lucy died last summer—you
ask me if I cry?
Hell, I'll show you tears, they're all
over this ground
They're falling from these blue
Alberta skies

But I'm going to ride forever
You can't keep horsemen in a cage
Should the angels call well it's only
then
I might pull in the reins

They tell me I'm an old man, they tell
me I am blind
They took my driver's license, this
house ain't far behind
I say jump back all you big suits
'cause you've got something wrong
I ain't gone, no I ain't gone
I am still breathing and I still have my
pride
And I have my memories, your life it
never dies
Like the wind that blows in thunder
Or the stallion on the fly, I got it all
And I'm standing tall underneath
these blue Alberta skies

...villain Francis Bolt who attempts an escape on his

...less reliable mechanical steed—an all-terrain vehicle.

And I'm going to ride forever
You can't keep horsemen in a cage
Should the angels call well it's only then
I might pull in the reins

So I say to all you old men don't let yourself get broke
If you think the world's gone crazy and it's
Scratching at your throat
It's time to dust off that old saddle, get it on a horse
Kick up your spurs, we're gonna run like stink
We're gonna tear across these blue Alberta skies

We're gonna ride forever
You can't keep horsemen in a cage
Should the angels call it's only then
I might pull in the reins

Written by Paul Gross and David Keeley.
Published by Don't Blink Music Inc.

The secret policeman's snow ball: Fraser falls by the edge of a cliff.
("The Edge")

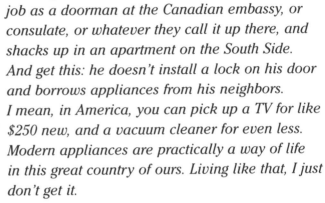

—how did I ever end up in this situation? I mean, sure, Fraser's a good guy and a great friend, but I don't get him sometimes. He comes to Chicago looking for his father's killer, gets a job as a doorman at the Canadian embassy, or consulate, or whatever they call it up there, and shacks up in an apartment on the South Side. And get this: he doesn't install a lock on his door and borrows appliances from his neighbors. I mean, in America, you can pick up a TV for like $250 new, and a vacuum cleaner for even less. Modern appliances are practically a way of life in this great country of ours. Living like that, I just don't get it.

I've been up there

—to Canada—a number of times, and it's cold. But that's not the worst part. At Fraser's he doesn't have a bathroom, and it's real thrilling running to the outhouse when you have to go. Haven't these Canadians heard of plumbing?

Being American means being as heavily armed as possible at all times. Cross the border, and they take away what we Americans know best—our guns. Fraser's been tooling around the mean streets of Chicago without a gun. What's that all about? All because he couldn't get a license for his sidearm. If I could get Fraser a license for his wolf, I certainly could get a license for his sidearm. But noooo, that would technically be breaking the law, and that's not the Canadian way of doing things. What upstanding citizens.

Speaking of upstanding, what's with Fraser and the Dragon Lady? I suspect something's going on and something is standing on guard for thee, but I can't quite put my finger on it. Canada produces some strong women, that's for sure.

Working with Dudley Do-Right has been fruitful, and Fraser does employ some unusual crime-fighting methods, like tasting dirt and sniffing doggie pid-dle. And then there was the time with the dead Russian spy: even when I was on assignment underground I heard about it from the other Ray. If that smelling thing isn't unusual, then what is? Fraser's tracking abilities are second to none, and he does seem to have a sixth sense when it comes to fighting crime. And despite my reservations about his crime-fighting techniques I've got to say that "he does get his man."

Splish splash I was having a bath: During one of their more interesting capers, Ray and Fraser find them-selves locked in a bank vault that is slowly filled with water. The door becomes a floodgate when blown open by bank robbers, and a torrent of water (along with Ray and Fraser) issues forth from the vault. Justice prevails! ("Vault")

The Riv

Ray's car and chief obsession is his 1971 green Buick Riviera, which he uses for work and in the pursuit of criminals. He spent years finding a replacement cigarette lighter for the car, although he doesn't smoke and never uses it. Fraser once discovered a sealed user's manual for the car in the glove compartment and unwrapped it. The car has been blown up and set on fire, but a replacement is always, thankfully, found.

Yeah, so I have this thing for Italian suits, but I don't like being called Detective Armani. Clothes are one of my only real indulgences besides free pizza and the occasional card game with the boys (God forbid that Fraser would gamble). And yes, I have an unnatural relationship with my car, a 1971 Buick Riviera. Fraser's managed to blow that up a few times in the course of crime fighting, though I seem to get replacements once in a while. Call it divine intervention—from a Canadian god no doubt.

Ray leans against his pride and joy: the 1971 Buick Riviera that he uses in the line of duty as his police car. During its crime-fighting career, the car has been blown up, abused in high-speed car chases, and used to transport semi-wild canines (and criminals) through the streets of Chicago and beyond.

- height: 6 feet (183 cm)

- weight: 165 pounds (75 kg)

- balding, with brown hair

- sixteen years on the job with the Chicago Police Department

- divorced from Angie, a policewoman; no children from the marriage. Ray and Angie are on speaking terms and share the services of the family mechanic, Al Grosso. Love interests have included Irene Zuko, ATF agent Suzanne Chaplin and state's attorney Louise St. Laurent

- lives with his mother, sisters Francesca and Maria, and brother-in-law Tony in a large house at 2926 N. Octavia Avenue, Chicago, that Ray inherited from his father

- Ray's elderly uncle Lorenzo lives in a dream world populated by gangsters and Al Capone. Ray has been known to consult Uncle Lorenzo on the ways of gangsters. Ray's other uncle, Angelo, is deceased

- assumed the role of father figure after his father's death — probably from alcoholism or a heart attack. Ray's father still appears as an apparition from time to time, to dispense (usually bad) advice to his son

These are just some of Vecchio's favorite things

- Free pizza
- Card games involving small wagers between players
- Pool games
- Sharp Italian Armani suits
- The Riv
- Florida vacations
- Donuts (what good cop doesn't like them?)

Reality Check
David Marciano

While David Marciano has moved on to other acting pastures, he continues to underpin the story of *Due South*, and will probably appear in future episodes as the fast-talking Italian cop when he comes up for air after being "deep, deep, under-cover." Marciano was born in Newark, New Jersey, and considered an acting career after failing to become a biomedical engineer. He has worked as an actor since 1983, appearing in such series as *Duet*, *China Beach*, *Touched by an Angel* and *The Last Don I and II*. His film credits include *Harlem Nights*, *Lethal Weapon II*, and *Come See the Paradise*.

RAY: Being an American, I also know where my strength lies, and that's in being as heavily armed as possible at all times.

ILLINOIS

RCW 139

LAND OF LINCOLN

Big Red meets Grizzly Adams: A clash of cultures and styles gets worked out in the boxing ring. ("Perfect Strangers")

Where's Smokey the Bear when you need him? Fraser and Ray arrive just in time to thwart the work of a performance arsonist. ("Burning Down the House")

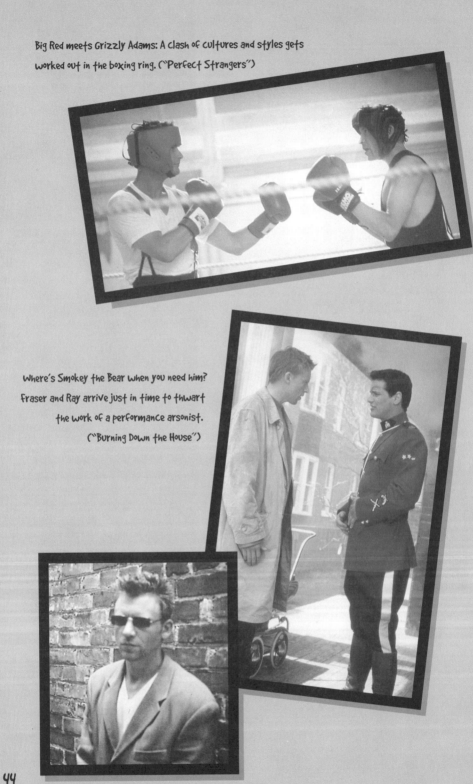

The Riv meets its ultimate fate and Stanley Kowalski becomes a new face on the force.

Reality Check
Callum
Keith Rennie

Born in England to Scottish parents and raised in Alberta, Rennie caught the acting bug for life after performing at the A.B.O.P. Theater in Edmonton. This was followed by a season at the Shaw Festival in Niagara-on-the-Lake, Ontario. Since then, Rennie has appeared in many roles, in shows that include *The X-Files*, *My Life as a Dog* and *For Those Who Hunt the Wounded Down*. In addition to his starring role next to Paul Gross in *Due South*, he can be seen in many Canadian and American feature films including *Mastermind*, *Hard Core Logo*, Don McKellar's *Last Night* and David Cronenberg's *eXistenZ*. He also co-starred in CBC's quixotic comedy *Twitch City*.

Ray Kowalski's Citations

December 1988: *for rescuing a young boy held hostage in warehouse. Ray drew fire and was wounded*

December 1990: *for holding off three gunmen in a jewelry store and saving four innocent lives in the face of danger*

September 1993: *for single-handedly facing down three escaped murderers and bringing them to justice*

- height: 5 feet 10 1/2 inches (178 cm)
- weight: 159 pounds (72 kg)
- sight: 20/45 vision
- tattoo on right shoulder
- education: graduated with a 61 percent average from high school
- marital status: divorced from State's Attorney Stella Kowalski
- keeps a pet turtle

> **This gig was supposed to be a chance to start over.**

But they didn't tell me I'd be teamed up with a freak. I can't get the goods on this gig from the other "real" Ray, who is now deep underground, investigating some deal for the Feds. Not only is it hard pretending to be Ray Vecchio, it's hard getting used to my new sidekick, Dudley Do-Right. You've got to give this Canajun a hand, though—he does seem to get his man.

The Ray charade has been interesting, to say the least. Take the dream catcher that Fraser gave me for my "birthday." The thing worked like a charm to get rid of one of my personal demons: the humiliation I suffered in front of my childhood sweetheart and future wife as the result of a scare I suffered during a bank robbery (I peed my pants from fright). Twenty-two years later Fraser appears on the scene during a stakeout in a graveyard while I'm on the lookout for the bank robber who scared the beejeezus out of me when I was a child. He convinces me that my former wife didn't care about that incident and it had nothing to do with why our marriage broke up. We were just kids when she witnessed the incident in the bank, and the trauma of having my future wife, Stella, see me lose control of my bladder during a moment of terror has haunted me in dreams to this day. When Fraser gave me the dream catcher made with eagle feathers that day, I flung it like a Frisbee and it spun and landed near the bank robber I blamed for the failure of my marriage. I'd found him with the help of the dream catcher, then met and defeated the demon from my past, and resolved what I believed to be the deep-rooted source of my problems. Fraser saw it differently: the bank robber had nothing to do with the breakdown, and the effect it had on me was way out of proportion with the emotional damage that I believed had been inflicted on me by the incident in the bank. The bank robber, now an old, tired man, didn't even remember me. He hadn't set out to ruin me for life. Fraser explained that I had just let the recollection of it spiral out of control in my mind, blaming the bank robber for my problems.

I guess it's sort of a complicated, emotional way to be introduced to a friend. Fraser is deeper than you'd think, and he has wisdom—you've got to respect that. But he's still a freak in many ways.

Why are you looking at us like that? Fraser and Ray discuss things in private. ("Eclipse")

w - o - l - f

It's a dog's life, if you have to know the truth.

I guess Fraser thinks he owes me something after I saved his life, pulling him from Prince Rupert Sound, and that's the reason he dotes on me the way he does. And just because my eardrums burst due to the water pressure, I realize it must be annoying to have to e-n-u-n-c-i-a-t-e every word.

Of course, that sometimes works to my advantage; taking orders isn't always the way to go. I've often wondered about my name, "Diefenbaker." Unless I'm getting my consonants confused, I know I growl, but that doesn't bear any relation to the jowls of my namesake, that geyser boss-man who looks more like a pug than a wolf. Humans are daft sometimes.

Since moving to Chicago, the pads on my feet have gotten smoother; the hard ground also plays havoc with my nails. The thing I don't get is that I can't roam free during the day without causing some kind of commotion. I'm not one of those sissy dogs on leashes in the park, you know, though I did fall for a beautiful bitch and got her "into trouble." Fraser took it well, considering. Sometimes at night I dream of being the lead sled dog (er, wolf), digging my paws into the unpacked snow as my pups and I pull Fraser towards our destination to the words "mush, mush" (if only I could still hear that word).

I do have visitation privileges, and Maggie's mistress has kind of taken a shine to Fraser. If only he would lick his coat clean and show more interest, then maybe Fraser could have pups too. But I guess that's not in the cards. Besides, the last time he tried to make pups I got hurt by his friend Victoria. Why does Fraser have to be so human? And please, take off that funny red suit.

Fraser says that every d-o-g has its day. But I'm not a d-o-g, I'm a w-o-l-f. That's a problem in Chicago, because Fraser had trouble getting a license for a w-o-l-f. Ray helped out with that one, but I still think my two-legged friends have some pretty funny rules. Sometimes they put other humans into cages. Ray and Fraser do that a lot, especially after humans fight. I know I have sharp teeth and humans don't have sharp teeth. They like to use firearms on each other. That's baffling. Anyway, when this Chicago mission is over, I'm going to look forward to the Great White North again.

Diefenbaker jumps the fence in an act of athletic agility. ("The Wild Bunch")

50

"It's becoming increasingly apparent, Dief, that maybe that woman's not for me." Fraser consoles Diefenbaker at the vet's after the wolf suffers near-fatal wounds. ("Victoria's Secret")

Diefenbaker in action again. Fraser would be in trouble without such an intelligent creature by his side. ("Dead Guy Running")

Fraser:
You know, you let a wolf save your life, and then you pay and you pay.

"You want to get that wolf away from my kid?" Oh, well, that's going to be difficult. He rarely does anything I ask him to. We've tried to work through it, God knows I've done my part, but it's something we can't seem to get past.
—Const. Benton Fraser on his wolf

- coloration: silver-gray with tan-colored legs; sometimes red, cream, tawny, buff

- hearing: acute; able to hear wolf calls from 6 to 10 miles away (10 to 16 km)

- teeth: forty-two, with four "canine" fangs that are about 1 1/4 inches (3.2 cm) long

- weight: 50 to 100 pounds (23 to 45 kg). Females weigh less than males. The largest wolves are found in the Yukon and can weigh up to 115 pounds (52 kg)

- speed: 0 to 35 MPH (0 to 56 kmph) with a cruising speed of 5 to 9 mph (8 to 14.5 kmph)

- weatherproofing: two fur coats — one thick undercoat and an overcoat. Wolves have the ability to withstand temperatures dipping as low as minus 50°F (-46°C)

- socialization: wolves travel in packs numbering between two and thirty, including extended family members and other wolves that attach themselves to the pack. Fraser and Diefenbaker form a pack

The proud mother and father: Maggie (left) and Diefenbaker (right) are responsible for siring a litter of young pups. Fraser took the news well. ("The Wild Bunch")

The Wolf's Namesake— Will the Real Diefenbaker Please Stand Up?

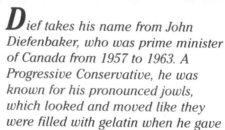

***D**ief takes his name from John Diefenbaker, who was prime minister of Canada from 1957 to 1963. A Progressive Conservative, he was known for his pronounced jowls, which looked and moved like they were filled with gelatin when he gave his impassioned political speeches denouncing the American influence on the Canadian way of life. His policies for northern Canada brought health care, education and other "civilizing" amenities to the Inuit, although these were later criticized for robbing the Native people of their traditional way of life. An initiative to preserve that way of life will result in the founding of a new Canadian territory, Nunavut ("Our Land" in Inuktitut), in 1999.*

Elaine Besbriss

I've got to say that when Fraser first appeared on the scene I was more than a little bit suspicious about what was going on. Let's face it: the cutest man that a woman ever did see steps into my life and treats everyone around him (including me) with manners, dignity and respect. I do love a man in a uniform—even if it happens to be red. And let's not forget that Fraser can type faster than I can, and that's saying a lot. I'm a sucker for uniforms and maybe that's why I ended up here doing police work and hoping that one day I might end up being a real law officer. Fraser would have been a catch, even with his assortment of peculiarities. But as fate would have it, nothing transpired between us, and I've been left to my own devices to carry on in my role as minion and faithful helper to Lieutenant Welsh, Ray, Fraser and the rest of the officers in the precinct.

I think Fraser and I think along the same lines and use the power of deduction and reasoning when investigating crimes. Ray's methods fall to the brash, while Fraser stands back and looks for underlying clues. That's another thing I respect: his patience and willingness to look beyond the obvious. He's also hell on wheels with a computer, and I've seen his fingers fly across a keyboard when he's in binary tracking mode. Seems like they teach some mean computer stuff up there in Canada.

elaine's reflections on Fraser:

I know what it is. I'm an idiot. I meet this guy, he's like no one I've ever met before. You know . . . warm, caring, sensitive . . . the kind that really rips your guts out. And right there I should have known. There should have been this big neon sign flashing in 10-foot-high letters: ELAINE, YOU'RE ABOUT To MAKE A COMPLETE FOOL OF YOURSELF!

I mean, just who the hell does he think he is? Coming around here with that dopey-looking grin, saying things like, "Good morning, Elaine." "How are you today Elaine?" "Thank you kindly for your time, Elaine." Like I'm supposed to take that?

And the minute you let him get to you, you can't sleep, your skin starts to break out, and the next thing you know you're wandering around supermarkets humming tunes by the Carpenters at the top of your lungs! Do you have any idea what that feels like?

Vital Statistics

- age: 27 to 29 years old (one of Elaine's best-kept secrets)
- dresses in relatively drab attire — a blue Civilian Aid uniform; rarely gets tarted up for work
- has brown hair and brown eyes
- seeks excitement beyond the job by eating ice cream
- personal life (like her age) is somewhat of a mystery as Elaine discloses little when she's on the job
- studied to be a real police officer; Francesca is now trying to fill Elaine's shoes as Civilian Aid

Reality Check
Catherine Bruhier

Catherine Bruhier is no theatrical lightweight. She studied drama at George Brown College, York University and the University of Toronto before setting out professionally. She has played leading roles in various productions across Canada, including the Shaw Festival in Niagara-on-the-Lake, Theatre Plus Toronto and the Toronto World Stage Festival. Her TV credits include ABC's *Knightwatch*, Warner Brothers' *Kung Fu: The Legend Continues*, CBS's *Top Cops*, *Shadowbuilder*, and *Forever Knight*.

Always a willing partner in Fraser's adventures, Elaine never complains about putting in extra work time, even if it means coming in on her night off. The Mountie's magnetic personality at work again?

Choosing a campsite sight unseen takes on new meaning for Fraser, who finds himself badly concussed and unable to see after the plane he was flying in crashes in the North. The first of what he believes to be hallucinations, where his late father appears to "help out," turns out to be Dad's return from the dead as an apparition. ("North")

Another of Francesca's plots to bed Fraser after choir practice unravels as the Mountie takes flight from the bevy of women behind him to pursue his first love: justice. ("The Deal")

Fraser and Thatcher embrace atop a speeding train, but it won't be until Thatcher is hot to trot that the two will earn their stripes as "mounted policemen." ("All the Queen's Horses")

Top 10 Episodes

"All the Queen's Horses"

A trainload of Mounties, Fraser, his boss Meg Thatcher, Sgt. "Buck" Frobisher, and a group of terrorists are interesting ingredients in this classically Canadian adventure. Disguised as a film crew shooting a documentary of the RCMP's famed equitation group of thirty-two horsemen, the Musical Ride, Fraser and his compadres do battle with a group of terrorists who take over the train that carries the Mounties on a trans-continental tour.

The terrorists gas the thirty-two members of the Musical Ride as they sing "Ride Forever," but Fraser, "Buck" Frobisher, and Meg Thatcher are left awake to contend with the hijacked train. Frobisher has personal gas problems to contend with, as well, after eating moose hock rolled in wild boar tongue and covered in gorgonzola cheese. In the tradition of Alfred Hitchcock, the heat of the moment throws Fraser and his boss Meg Thatcher into an embrace atop the hijacked train as it heads for a tunnel. The romance comes to an abrupt end when Fraser and Thatcher are captured and Fraser is forced into reading the terrorists' ransom demands. Frobisher, with the help of Fraser's ghostly father, is left to his own devices to save the train filled with sleeping Mounties from impending disaster. But Fraser and Thatcher manage to free themselves and to stop the train. Realizing that their plot has unraveled, the terrorists attempt to flee, but the now-awakened members of the Musical Ride take to their horses and round up the terrorists and ringleader Randall Bolt.

Inspector

I really like my creature comforts: spas, vacations, that kind of thing. When I accepted the posting in Chicago, I didn't expect to be put in charge of a Mountie with a mission, though I've come to accept that it goes with the territory – being Canadian, that is. It's our birthright to defend Queen and country, and Fraser's taken that to mean even when we're in another's country. I suppose that's what motivates our favorite Mountie, who takes crime-fighting really seriously. Fraser's doing wonderful things for international relations by joining up with the Chicago law-enforcement authorities, but I'm glad he's doing it on his own time, and dime.

Benton's a curiosity to me, and I've been drawn to him in rather delicate ways, if you understand my meaning. I made a promise to myself that I would never get involved with a subordinate, but I've gone and broken that rule, as you well know. It was definitely the heat of the moment, if you could call standing atop a train moving at 100 kilometers an hour in the middle of winter a "hot" moment. In any event, I lost my composure and kissed Benton's delicious mouth for several delicious minutes.

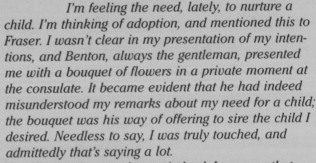

I didn't expect to be put in charge of a Mountie with a mission

I've not quite recovered from that professionally, and emotionally … well, I can't seem to scare away the thought of the two of us entwined in each other's arms as we make passionate love in front of a crackling fire. A Canadian idea of romance, I presume. But that's the truth of the matter.

I'm feeling the need, lately, to nurture a child. I'm thinking of adoption, and mentioned this to Fraser. I wasn't clear in my presentation of my intentions, and Benton, always the gentleman, presented me with a bouquet of flowers in a private moment at the consulate. It became evident that he had indeed misunderstood my remarks about my need for a child; the bouquet was his way of offering to sire the child I desired. Needless to say, I was truly touched, and admittedly that's saying a lot.

Benton is a gentleman indeed. I suppose that harlot Francesca will continue attempting to lure him into her boudoir. I'm hoping that Fraser will continue to exercise restraint, along with a modicum of discrimination, when it comes to Francesca. But why should I be so concerned? I'm not laying claim to Benton, and I have certainly resisted further affairs of the heart with him. If only I could banish him from my thoughts.

Vital Statistics

- wears reading glasses and has the body and legs to accommodate short skirts; owns a red serge Mountie uniform and wears it on formal occasions

- height: about 5 feet, 6 inches (168 cm)

- recently changed her image by trimming her shoulder-length hair

- a no-nonsense woman who has disappointed herself by fraternizing romantically with a subordinate (Const. Fraser)

Reality check
Camilla Scott

A talk-show host, singer and dancer, Camilla Scott commands a solid reputation as a stage actress, appearing in such productions as *Crazy for You*. Her television credits include playing the character Melissa Anderson on the NBC soap *Days of Our Lives*. She has appeared in various other TV shows, including *Top Cops*, *Alfred Hitchcock Presents*, *Friday the 13th* and *Robocop*. Her movie credits include *Three Men and a Baby*. She appears in the animated series *The X-Men* as the voice of Lillandra and as the voice of Shalla Ball in the animated series *Silver Surfer*.

"Victoria's Secret"

Fraser's composure crumbles when his first true love, Victoria Metcalfe, appears as if from a dream in the Mountie's new life in Chicago, and what starts out as a good dream quickly becomes a nightmare as Fraser is drawn into a web of deceit and illusory emotions. Bound by the law, Fraser was forced to turn Victoria in after she and her partner Jolly pulled off a bank robbery many years earlier. Now free from jail, Victoria appears unexpectedly in Chicago and rekindles Fraser's feelings for her. The feelings are, unfortunately, not mutual and it becomes apparent to Ray (and everyone else except Fraser) that Victoria has other things on her mind. When Diefenbaker ends up shot and Fraser gets arrested for passing marked bills, Victoria emerges as the villain. To complicate matters, Fraser and Ray discover that Jolly is pursuing Victoria to reclaim money from the bank heist that sent Victoria to jail. When Jolly dies in a shootout, the Mountie believes that Victoria shot Jolly in self defense. But there are no witnesses and Victoria has disappeared. In a final, parting moment Fraser bids farewell to the woman he still loves after finding her at the train station, but not before he comes between a bullet and Victoria that has been fired to stop her escape.

The Ladies Spar Off

thatcher:
You know, the uniform, the motion, the legs ... driving like pistons, pumping like steel.

francesca:
I know exactly what you mean.

thatcher:
I doubt it. Nevertheless, this was obviously not a crime of logic. It was a crime of passion.

francesca:
Oh, like in *Sword of Desire*. It's this great book I'm reading about this guy who has this huge ...

opportunity knocks for Francesca: Is this her big chance to skin the object of her desire and get a peek at Fraser's night stick? Sister Maria is there to witness the action. ("They Eat Horses, Don't They?")

I've tried and I've tried and I've tried—

and still can't seem to bag or bed Fraser. I thought that by filling the position of Civilian Aid left vacant by Elaine, I would be able to get closer to Fraser by volunteering in the office. Talking to a Mountie from Canada is kinda like talking to a priest. I mean, not that I think of Fraser as a priest, 'cause you know I don't. I think of him as a man. It's that priests can't do certain things. I've tried lingerie, showed up at the guy's door, and made it so obvious that I'm crazy about him. But still no real results. What is this guy, invincible or something?

Anyhow, now that I'm bettering myself by signing on with the Chicago PD, he might take more notice. And anyway, I'm closer to him than I ever was, not to mention that I get to feast my eyes on this supreme example of maleness sent, no doubt, from heaven above to taunt and tease women like me. Since I can't count on my bonehead brother to put in a good word for me on the Fraser front, I'll try and implicate myself into Fraser's life the best I can, and the volunteer job at the precinct has at least put me in constant contact with Fraser. I'm not so good with computers, but both Fraser and Elaine have been patient. The extra attention I get from time to time is ample reward for putting up with the long hours and no pay.

Reality Check
Ramona Milano

A professional actress since the age of 17, Milano began her career straight out of drama school with a stint as a singer/dancer at Canada's Wonderland amusement park. Later gigs included entertaining the Canadian Armed Forces overseas, singing on a cruise boat and acting in the stage production of *One Flew Over the Cuckoo's Nest*. She recently appeared in *The Last Don*, *The Absolute Truth* and had a guest-starring role on *Traders*.

Some of Francesca's Favorite Things

- lingerie from Frederick's of Hollywood
- romance novels, including Harlequin Romances; books by Danielle Steele and Jackie Collins are also favorites
- hairspray and styling gel, resulting in "big hair" hairdos
- velour clothing; tastes lean towards chintz
- has traveled to New York's Long Island, which she considers heaven on earth

Lt. Harding Welsh

I'm getting a little old for the fun and games that have been going on around the precinct over the past few years. It all started with the arrival of that red angel from Canada. It was hard enough keeping up with the shenanigans of my regular detectives, let alone the real, original hijinks that the Mountie introduced with his arrival on the scene. On a professional level I understand his motivation for wanting to fight crime, but what I don't get is, the guy already has a job at the consulate and then donates his time to a foreign country's police force.

I was going to put my foot down when he began working with a reluctant Vecchio, but the aggravation demonstrated by my more hot-headed detective made it worth enduring this unusual experiment in international relations. What I didn't want was to have the situation hit the papers. I've had enough trouble with meddling politicians, and the last thing I needed was to have any publicity around the situation, especially with Cahill constantly breathing down my back. Mind you, when the Mountie teamed up with Vecchio in the beginning, our crime-solving stats improved dramatically and the Mountie began to make the precinct look good—too good, in some ways. The Mountie's a whiz on computers and introduced my boys to some rather unusual investigative techniques. Vecchio told me that the Mountie once crawled around like a dog sniffing out the trail of his canine companion, Diefenbaker.

Things really got wacky around here, and when Vecchio was seconded by Justice for a top-secret mission, bringing the "new Ray" up to speed on the situation here was a bit, well, difficult, to put it mildly. I mean, how do you tell a professional cop that he'll be shadowed by a man in a red uniform? There are jokes about guys like that. Kowalski took it pretty well, considering, but I think he's still getting used to having Constable Fraser as his unofficial "official" partner. I heard Kowalski call him a "freak." Maybe, but those Canucks are all a bit kooky when you come right down to it. They're dismissive of our right to bear arms and some other things that are near and dear to our hearts. Never mind that they insist on occupying a country that's frigidly cold most of the year and inhospitable to life, for the most part.

Lt. Harding Welsh Dossier

- age: about 55 years old
- height: 6 feet 3 inches (190 cm)
- weight: about 235 pounds (107 kg)
- near-sighted; requires glasses for reading
- heads up the Violent Crimes Unit of the Chicago PD
- frequently runs up against other federal crime-fighting organizations, which tends to frustrate his efforts to fight crime at "the street level"

Reality check
Beau Starr

Gruff and to the point on *Due South*, this is one guy you shouldn't mess with. Beau Starr's impressive physical stature harks back to a football career where he played for the Montreal Alouettes in 1969 and the Hamilton Tiger Cats in 1970. Starr was born in Queens, New York, and attended Hofstra University, where he earned a B.A. in biology. He currently resides in Burbank, California, and his recent screen credits include *While My Pretty One Sleeps* and *F/X: The Series*.

Ray and a perplexed Lt. Welsh look on while Huey reluctantly puts the cuffs on Fraser after the Mountie is framed for passing numbered bills.

(a.k.a. "Huey")

*W*asn't that long ago that I didn't like the boy in red from Canada. He and Ray made the rest of us look bad because their rate of success in solving crimes was nearly 100 percent, while mine and Louie's was only around 60 percent. But I've grown to like the fellow, and can appreciate his methods a bit better now. The Mountie looks at the big picture and analyzes the whole situation. Me, I'm a detail person who likes to put the little things together like I was putting together a puzzle.

I put our differences in approach down to our different upbringings and experience. When you're charging through the snow on a dog-drawn sleigh like Santa, that's got to make you different from someone like me, who's used to charging around a big city in a fast car. I'd say one uses their wits a bit more on the tundra and looks for clues that are out of the ordinary.

Louie and I came to like the Mountie, but that was cut short by Louie's untimely death. My new partner seems to appreciate Fraser, though you'd have to ask him what he thought coming into the job.

funeral for a friend:
Pallbearers carry Det.
Louis Gardino's casket.
("Juliet is Bleeding")

Reality Check
Tony Craig

As well as being a recognized actor with roles in *Hoover vs. the Kennedys*, *Top Cops*, *Forever Knight* and *Scales of Justice* (directed by David Cronenberg), Tony Craig is an accomplished musician. With numerous recordings to his credit, he has sung and drummed next to bands and musicians ranging from Rough Trade to Dan Hill.

The end of the road for Ray Vecchio's 1971 Buick
Riviera and for Det. Louis Gardino.
("Juliet is Bleeding")

DET. LOUIS GARDINO

(a.k.a. "Louie")

Status: Deceased/Killed in a car explosion

Top 10 Episodes

"North"

Fraser and Ray end up as sorry boy scouts in this adventure that pits Fraser's advanced wilderness survival skills against the forces of the criminal mind. Merrily on their way to the "ultimate Canadian vacation," Fraser and Ray's plane is hijacked by an escaped convict who crashes the plane in a remote woods. Fraser suffers injuries in the crash and loses his eyesight. But intent on "getting his man," Fraser insists on using his remaining senses to outwit the escaped convict despite Ray's misgivings. Without food and weapons, Fraser and Ray are at their wits' end as their respective fathers appear as apparitions and offer unusual advice to each of their sons. But despite Fraser's weakened state, Ray's inexperience in the wilderness, and each of their father's weird advice, the crime-fighters triumph and bring justice to the wilds of Canada.

*F*illing Louie's shoes is a bit of a hard act to follow, especially since they're dead man's shoes. And I have none of the history that goes along with working for years at the precinct. When I first got here, there was this crackpot wearing a red Mountie uniform floating around. The kind of nut bar that police departments sometimes attract. I asked my new partner about this and he presented me with the facts: a loonie-tunes Canadian crime-fighter who enjoys spending his spare time helping us out here in Chicago is now Stanley Kowalski's unofficial "official" partner. I've watched a few of his moves, and I've got to say he uses some pretty advanced investigative techniques. He and Kowalski are hell on ice when it comes to solving crimes.

Vital Statistics

age: 34 to 35 years old
weight: 175 pounds (79 kg)
hair color: brown
eye color: brown
place of birth: Chicago

Sgt. Buck Frobisher

Sgt. Duncan "Buck" Frobisher is a legend among men, particularly men of the RcMP. ("All the Queen's Horses")

Fraser and Frobisher are ages apart but share a love of horses and equestrian events.

sgt. buck frobisher:

I like to think that there's a little Hamlet in all of us. Not that melancholy stuff. Or being a prince. But I've always believed that we should have a little Danish in us. Especially in the morning.

remember when the lad was born.

It was a momentous occasion for Bob, but he always felt the lad should learn to pry his way through life by himself. After Caroline passed on, God bless her soul, Bob turned the boy over for his education to his parents. Fraser turned out—if turning out is the right way to describe things—to be a good boy indeed. It was good to see father and son united again that time on the train. Bob hasn't aged a bit, but then again, how could he age when he's dead? That's a good question to ponder.

Life seems to go in circles. Take Geiger, for instance. I was stabbed in the leg by Geiger and then, in turn, Fraser was also stabbed by the villain. Both the boy and I will now suffer the same painful ailment and remember the incidents every time the wound aches for the rest of our living days. It is as if the ache returns like an old friend who comes for tea and biscuits only in times of dampness and bad weather. Some would say a fair weather friend, or more precisely, a bad weather friend. Whatever kind of friend, the cyclical nature of life and its incumbent irritations is something that we all share, particularly if one is a member of the Royal Canadian Mounted Police.

Poor old Robert, if only I could have been on the scene when those jackals rubbed him out. His expiration was untimely and I would have enjoyed another game of cards with him, if that was in the cards. It's as though we all have an expiry date stamped somewhere on our souls. Which makes me wonder when I'll go bad.

```
Sgt. Buck Frobisher Dossier

• age: early sixties
• height: 6 feet (183 cm)
• hair: completely gray
• manner: distracted at times;
demeanor suggests a man completely
at home with himself
• captured notorious killer Harold
Geiger
• is a career Mountie with well
over 40 years on the force
```

Naked Gun IV: Frobisher jumps on a police motorcycle and pops a wheelie before going after the villain Geiger. ("Manhunt")

Cultural Equivalents

*W*hat country am I in? We look the same, speak the same language, and act the same (sort of), but scratch the surface and you'll find profound differences between Yanks and Canucks. Here's a quick action guide to figuring out what's going on when crossing the 49th parallel—in both directions.

United States	Canada
Newsweek	Maclean's
Congress	Parliament
credit	deficit
capital gains	taxation
HMOs	universal health care
baseball	curling
American	English
FBI	RCMP
McCloud	Fraser
bald eagle	beaver
embassy	high commission
Texas	Quebec
ABC	CBC
the right to bear arms	gun control
L.L. Bean	Roots
Harley-Davidson	Ski-Doo
miles	kilometers
theater	theatre
Ronald Reagan	Brian Mulroney
$1.00	69¢
greenback	loonie
restroom	washroom

A truly patriotic choice: Which wires in which order will disarm the bomb tied to Ray and Fraser by Bolt? Hint: What are old Glory's colors? ("Red, White, and Blue")

"Letting Go"

With time on his hands while recovering in hospital after being shot and nursing a broken heart after his painful parting with Victoria in "Victoria's Secret," Fraser becomes curious about the activities that are staged in the office windows that face his hospital room. Fraser's injuries prevent him from personally investigating what he believes are misdeeds taking place in the windows opposite his hospital room but he finds a willing—and able—partner in his physical therapist Jill Kennedy.

Replaying the turn of events in the classic thriller *Rear Window*, Fraser sends Jill in to the offices opposite the hospital to investigate. Soon Ray and Diefenbaker are also involved, but it is Fraser who saves the day when he takes to his crutches and comes to the rescue.

insp. moffat ("the pilot"):

These are Americans, Fraser. If they think they can walk all over you, they will. It's a delicate balance; you have to be just as shrewd, cunning and ruthless as they are. And then, being Canadians, we have to be polite.

Identifying Americans

pilot (to fraser):

They were all wearing new boots, they were driving a Jeep Wrangler, and they carried big guns.

fraser:

Americans it is.

73

Scrapbook

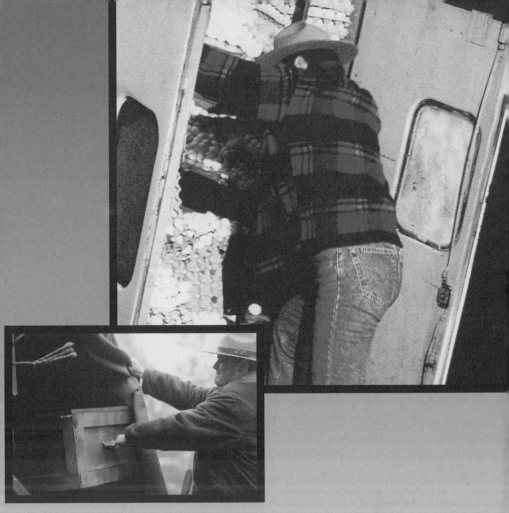

Identifying Canadians

mama Vecchio:
He's ... so polite.

ray Vecchio:
He's Canadian, Ma.

mama Vecchio:
Oh, I thought he was sick or something.

*T*his backcountry recipe is renowned by voyagers as a quick way to fill up on the trail, whether it's in the Canadian wilderness after your plane goes down, or as the main meal of the day after a hard day's canoeing on remote rivers and streams. Whatever and wherever, this gut-filling stuff will plug a hungry maw in minutes.

Bannock

5 cups (1 1/4 L) flour

9 tsp. (45 mL) baking powder   dash salt

3 1/2 (875 mL) cups water

Combine ingredients in a large bowl and add water while stirring quickly with a spoon until the mixture is smooth. Then put the ingredients into a greased frying pan. Place the frying pan on a level cooking grate over hot coals. The bannock is ready when no dough sticks to the tangs of a fork when inserted in the middle of the mixture and extracted.

Pizza

*R*ay Vecchio's taste for pizza is not a secret, though his whereabouts these days is. In fact, most cops of Italian heritage on the Chicago PD are more addicted to the things than doughnuts. Ray tries to get his for nothing by calling on pizza joints that promise to deliver in 30 minutes or less or the pizza is free. Call him cheap, but there are only so many ways to stretch a cop's salary, and this is one of them. When funds are low, Mama Vecchio can always be relied on to produce a beautiful, steaming mélange of cheese, tomato, sauce and pepperoni served up on a crisp crust. Mama likes her boys to eat, and Fraser has, over the years, become an honorary member of the Vecchio family.

Pizza Crust

3 tbsp. (45 mL) yeast

1/2 tsp. (2.5 mL) sugar

3/4 cup (185 mL) warm water

1 3/4 cups (435 mL) flour

Pinch of salt

Splash of vegetable oil

Combine the yeast, sugar and water in a medium-sized bowl and put aside for about 15 minutes, until foam appears on the mixture surface, and then stir the mixture again.

Measure out the flour and salt in another mixing bowl, then add the liquid mixture of yeast, sugar and water to the flour a little at a time while kneading the ingredients together by hand. Knead until all the ingredients are combined, working the dough into a sticky ball.

Sprinkle flour lightly over a flat surface. Flatten the dough by throwing it down hard on the surface. Continue to knead the dough for several minutes, sprinkling flour as needed over the cooking surface to prevent the dough from sticking until the dough is smooth and dry.

Then form the dough into a ball and place it in a lightly oiled bowl to rise (the bowl should be at least twice as big as the dough ball). Cover the bowl with a clean, dampened cloth and wait for about one hour, or until the dough has doubled in size.

Sprinkle flour onto your hands, place the dough in the middle of a 14-inch (36 cm) pizza pan, and then stretch the dough so that it conforms to the circular-shaped pan.

Tomato Sauce

1 large can crushed Roma tomatoes
(28 oz./840 g)

1/2 can tomato paste (approx.)

1 clove garlic

Pinch of salt

About 1/2 tsp. (2.5 mL) freshly ground pepper

Pinch of oregano

3 tbsp. (45 mL) crushed, dried basil leaves

1/2 tbsp. (8 mL) crushed, dried chili-pepper flakes

Finely chop garlic in a food processor or by hand with a knife, then stir the garlic and other ingredients together with the crushed tomatoes in a large bowl. Add tomato paste and mix until the sauce is not too thin.

Toppings

Any number of favorite ingredients may be used to dress up the crust. Canadians like Fraser have been known to spread lichen and moss over a bed of tomato sauce, or to shred freshly caught salmon over a lightly oiled crust of seal blubber. (That's according to Ray, but he may or may not be kidding.) The following is a favorite from Mama's recipe book.

Spread pizza sauce evenly over the crust, then sprinkle about 3/4 cup (185 mL) of shredded mozzarella over the sauce. Cover the sauce with 15 to 20 thin slices of hot pepperoni. Add other favorite toppings such as onion slices, artichoke hearts, green peppers or fried bacon, if desired.

Baking Instructions - Pizza

Place the pizza in an oven preheated to 500° F (260° C) and bake for 10 to 15 minutes until the cheese has thoroughly melted. Remove from the oven and serve.

*A*nother of Mama's favorite recipes, this pasta soup is a showstopper that sticks to the ribs on long, cold nights in the New World.

Pasta Fagioli (pasta and bean soup)

2 cans (28 oz./840 g each) white beans	2 1/2 quarts water
4 oz. (125 mL) olive oil	2 cans (28 oz. each) crushed Romano tomatoes
2 onions, chopped	1/4 lb. (115 g) small pasta
2 carrots, chopped	Grated Parmesan for garnish
1 celery stalk	Salt
1/4 lb. ham, chopped	Pepper

Drain the beans and rinse them thoroughly in sieve or large strainer. Sauté the onions, olive oil, carrots, celery and ham for 5 to 10 minutes in a medium-sized stockpot, until they are soft. Add the beans, water and tomatoes to the pot and bring to a boil, stirring constantly. Lower the heat, cover and simmer for about 2 hours; remove lid and stir periodically.

Use a food processor to purée half of the soup and add it back into the pot (leave half the soup unpuréed); take care when transferring the hot soup between the food processor and the pot.

Carefully add the pasta to the pot, turn up the heat and cook for another 10 to 15 minutes, stirring constantly. Then turn down the heat to low. Season to taste with salt and pepper, and ladle into bowls. Sprinkle Parmesan over the soup. If soup thickens, add water.

A rancher's staple, the following recipe is derived from the original hardy version that traditionally fed legions of cowboys and trailblazers who cooked over an open fire.

Baked Beans

3 cups (750 mL) navy beans	1/2 cup (125 mL) stewed tomatoes
3/4 cup (185 mL) brown sugar	3 teaspoons (15 mL) dry mustard
3/4 cup (185 mL) molasses	Pinch of salt
1/2 teaspoon (2.5 mL) instant coffee	3/4 pound (340 g) cubed salt port or side bacon
(1/2 cup/125 mL black coffee)	

Rinse the navy beans thoroughly in cold water and transfer them to a large pot. Soak the beans in water overnight. On the following day, add enough water to cover the beans again and bring the water to a boil. Cook until the beans are tender (about 1 hour). Drain the beans and place them in a large casserole dish. Add the remaining ingredients, along with enough water to cover the beans. Bake uncovered for 5 to 6 hours at 300° F (150° C). Periodically check the beans, adding more water as necessary to prevent them from drying out.

*W*ithout refrigeration and with a desire for meat while on the trail, Native peoples and early pioneers devised a way of preserving meat by drying it for later eating. "Jerky," as it came to be known, remains a popular snack food and can be made from any of a variety of meats.

Jerky

12 pounds (5.5 kg) lean red meat	
10 cups (2.5 L) water	
1 cup (250 L) coarse salt	1 1/2 tablespoons (23 mL) saltpeter
	1 teaspoon (5 mL) garlic powder
	3/4 teaspoon (4 mL) onion powder

Cut the meat into strips that are about 1 1/2 inches (3.8 cm) thick and trimmed of all excess fat. Place the meat in a freezer and leave it until firm. Use a boning knife to cut the pieces into very thin slices. Combine the remaining ingredients in a large bowl and immerse the meat slices in the mixture of water, salt, saltpeter, garlic powder and onion powder. Leave to sit for about an hour. After an hour, remove the slices and dry them by patting with a paper towel or a clean, dry cloth.

Put the meat slices across the grids of oven racks and place within an oven heated to 150° F (65° C) for 12 to 14 hours. Avoid cooking the meat; the meat should be placed no closer than 4 inches (10 cm) from the oven's heating element or flame and a pan should be placed on the bottom of the oven to catch fat that may cook off the meat. The jerky is done when the strips snap into two pieces when bent. Store refrigerated in sealed plastic bags.

RECIPES

*A*fter a hearty Canadian meal, voyageurs, trappers and other outdoors-folk looked forward to a delectable, filling meal followed by a rich dessert. In bygone days little or no thought was given to the waistline, and a hearty meat-based main course followed by a sugar-laden dessert was thought to be a fitting reward for enduring a day of bad, cold weather and back-breaking work. Traditional recipes such as tourtière and sugar pie, or tarte au sucre, are still enjoyed by those living in French Canada, especially in the wintertime when the body calls for extra energy to combat the cold.

Crust

1 cup (250 mL) soft butter (or other preferred shortening)

2 cups (500 mL) flour

2 to 6 tablespoons (30 to 90 mL) cold water

Add butter or shortening to the flour in the bowl by working it in with a fork or pastry tool until the mixture is coarse in texture. Gradually sprinkle water into the mixture, working it in with the fork as you do. Avoid adding too much water, and strive for a dough with a smooth consistency. Divide the dough into two equal pieces, one for making the pie bottom and the other for the top.

Sprinkle flour over a clean, dry cooking surface and use a rolling pin to flatten one piece of the dough into a roughly circular shape. Curl the dough over the rolling pin to lift it off the rolling surface and transfer it to a pie tin. Repeat the process for the pie top and cover the pie once it is filled with ingredients. Finish the edge of the pie by pressing the top and bottom together with the tongs of a fork all around the pie's circumference. For a fancier top, such as the one used for a sugar pie, slice the flattened dough into 1 1/2- to 2-inch (4 to 5 cm) slices and lay the slices individually over the top of the pie to make "lattice-top" pie.

Sugar Pie

4 cups (1 L) brown sugar (or maple sugar)

3 tablespoons (45 mL) heavy cream

2 tablespoons (30 mL) butter

Preheat the oven to 400° F (200° C). Combine brown sugar, cream and butter in a bowl and fill a 9-inch (23 cm) uncooked pie shell with the mixture using a spoon. Top the pie with strips of dough to make a "lattice-top" pie. Bake for 35 to 40 minutes, until the top of the pie is just slightly brown.

Seal Flipper Pie

2 seal flippers
3 slices salt pork fat
2 onions
1 turnip

2 carrots
1 parsnip
6 potatoes
Salt and pepper to taste

Cut off fat from flippers, rinse, and cut meat into 1-inch (2.5 cm) cubes. Fry the salt pork in a medium-sized baking pot until it is crisp; remove the fried pork "scruncheons" from the oil. Use the oil to brown the flipper cubes, and then add water and simmer until the flipper meat is tender.

Chop up the onions, turnip, carrots and parsnip, and add them to the meat. Cook for about 30 minutes. Add the potatoes and cook for another 15 minutes; add more water if needed.

Meanwhile, prepare a crust (recipe above). Once the flippers and vegetables are cooked, cover the mixture with a crust and bake at 425° F (220° C) for 20 minutes, or until nicely browned.

Moose Stew

3 pounds (1.4 kg) moose meat
1/4 pound (115 g) butter
6 cups (1.5 L) water
Salt and pepper to taste

2 carrots, peeled and chopped
2 parsnips
1 small turnip
10 potatoes

Cut up the moose meat into small pieces. Brown the meat in hot butter in the bottom of a large cooking pot. Add water, salt and pepper, cover the pot and simmer for about an hour. Chop the carrots, parsnips, turnip and potatoes and add them to the pot; simmer the vegetables and the meat together for another 30 minutes or until the vegetables are tender.

Tourtière

2 pounds (900 g) lean, ground pork
1 pound (450 g) ground beef
3 large potatoes, mashed
1 large, ground onion

Pepper and salt to taste
1/2 teaspoon (2.5 mL) cinnamon
1/2 teaspoon (2.5 mL) cloves
2 cups (500 mL) water

Cook the meat in a large pot of water for about an hour. Add onion and seasonings and cook at low heat for another 15 minutes or so. Add the mashed potatoes to the mixture and allow to cool. Use a large mixing spoon to fill a 9-inch (23 cm) crust (recipe above). Lay on a top crust. Pierce the middle of the pie top with a fork and bake at 400° F (200° C) for 30 minutes. Remove and allow to cool before serving.

WANTED
BY THE RCMP

Name: Ian MacDonald
Height: 5 feet 10 inches (178 cm)
Weight: 175 pounds (79 kg)
RCMP File: 97GE663

A convicted perjurer and a pathological liar. Testified in the trial of Canadian crime boss by the name of Danny Brock, who allegedly intimidated MacDonald into altering his testimony, resulting in a mistrial. Extradited to Canada and jailed for perjury.

Case status: Case Closed. MacDonald now paroled.

WANTED
BY THE RCMP

Name: Harold Geiger
Height: 6 feet 1 inch (185 cm)
Weight: 215 pounds (98 kg)
RCMP File: 99GE673

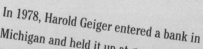

In 1978, Harold Geiger entered a bank in Michigan and held it up at gunpoint. A guard was shot by Geiger; the police and Federal Bureau of Investigation subsequently pursued Geiger across five states, before he headed north into Canada. In hot pursuit of the convicted felon, two FBI agents, a state trooper and a highway patrolman were murdered by Geiger. Once within Canada's borders, Geiger continued the melee, killing a police officer, two provincial police officers and two of the RCMP's Emergency Response team. Sgt. Buck Frobisher of the RCMP brought Geiger to justice after tracking him up to Whitehorse, where the officer was stabbed by Geiger in the leg. Geiger was subsequently tried and convicted, serving his sentence at White Island Maximum Security Prison, NWT.

Case Status: Case Closed.

"Manhunt"

Fraser's boyhood hero and his father's best friend, Sgt. Duncan "Buck" Frobisher, goes missing a week before retirement. Frobisher's distrught daughter Julie appears on the scene in Chicago and reveals that Frobisher has crossed the border from Canada and is in town. Fraser tracks Frobisher down and finds him hiding in a cheap hotel on the south side of town. When Fraser finds out that Frobisher's arch enemy, Harold Geiger, who Frobisher arrested thirty years ago, is on the lam, he joins forces with Frobisher to track Geiger down.

Games in *Due South*

Bobbing for Trout

Kick the Cabbage

Poker

Pool

Top 10 Episodes

In this case involving rancid meat and food poisoning Fraser and Ray are taken from the aisles of the supermarket to the insides of a slaughter house in their quest for the answer to why a pound of ground chuck smells like a mixture of black angus and quarterhorse. Foul meat turns to foul play when Fraser and Ray discover that criminals are slaughtering horses and selling the meat as beef. The criminals don't take kindly to being found out and lock Fraser and Ray in a meat locker to freeze to death. In order to survive the cold, Fraser employs an unusual Inuit technique to stay warm: he and Ray don animal carcasses.

WANTED
BY THE RCMP

Name: Victoria Metcalfe
Height: 5 feet 1 inch (155 cm)
Weight: 115 pounds (52 kg)
RCMP File: 95GE753

Victoria Metcalfe was convicted of bank robbery and served her sentence after being apprehended by Const. Benton Fraser, who tracked her into the mountains of a remote Canadian region. Once there, Const. Fraser and the subject were caught in a heavy snowstorm for four days. Const. Fraser's superior survival skills saved both lives, and the subject was brought to justice. Subsequently paroled, Metcalfe traveled to Chicago to complete some unfinished business. Const. Fraser, now working in Chicago, was injured by friendly fire as he attempted to apprehend the fleeing Metcalfe.

Case Status: Victoria Metcalfe remains at large. Considered armed and dangerous: Take no action to apprehend this person yourself; report any information to the nearest RCMP detachment or the police in your area.

WANTED BY THE RCMP

Name: Francis Bolt
Height: 5 feet 9 inches (175 cm)
Weight: 175 pounds (79 kg)
RCMP File: 97GE254

Francis Bolt, the brother of Randall Bolt—who was charged with two counts of murder in the first degree, one count of attempted murder, one count of possession of a controlled or illegal substance, hijacking, thirty-two counts of assault, and advocacy to overthrow the government of the United States of America by force or violence—staged a bold attempt to abduct his brother during his trial. Francis Bolt wired bombs to Const. Benton Fraser of the RCMP (who arrested his brother) and the Chicago Police Department's Det. Ray Vecchio, as well as dozens of other officers of the court. Both Francis and Randall Bolt were apprehended and turned over to federal authorities in the U.S.

Case Status: Case Closed.

Aurora Borealis a luminous phenomenon occurring in the Northern Hemisphere and caused by the planet's magnetic fields. Also called the *northern lights*.

Bannock a filling backcountry recipe, with the main ingredient being flour, that can be made over a campfire in a pan.

Bindlestitch a tool used by shoemakers for lifting laces off leather, described as having a curved head and a sharp point resembling a hook, measuring about six inches (15 cm) and used to catch sockeye salmon

Blackpot a verb used to describe the use of a new camping pan or pot to cook food over an open campfire. The new pot turns black from the carbon escaping from the fire's flames as they lick against the metal surface of the pot.

Glossary of Due South Terms

Gee the instruction from the human operator of a dogsled to running dogs up front to veer right (*also see* Haw, Mush *and* Stop!)

Haw the instruction from the human operator of a dogsled to running dogs up front to veer left (*also see* Gee, Mush *and* Stop!)

Inukshuk a "human" figure made of balanced stone slabs, believed to embody a human spirit. The Inukshuk is a constant element in Inuit art.

Inuktitut the traditional language of the Inuit peoples. The word means "to sound like Inuk." Inuktitut has been spoken for thousands of years but has been written only in recent years, after missionaries in the North developed a syllabic representation of the language.

Lichen green, gray or yellow fungus that typically grows on rocks in the Territories and is reputed to be used as pizza topping by Benton Fraser

Mush the instruction from the human operator of a dogsled to running dogs up front to go forward, with the effect of propelling the sled forward (*also see* Gee, Haw *and* Stop!)

Musical Ride early members of the Royal Canadian Mounted Police (RCMP) devised this colorful display of equestrian skills to the sound of music as a unique way to amuse themselves and to entertain the local community. The first musical ride was performed at the Regina barracks in 1897.

Musk-ox (*ovibos moschatus*) a large, woolly animal that makes its home in remote, barren areas of northern North America. The musk-ox is described by RCMP officers living in proximity to these animals as "foul smelling."

Mukluk an Inuit snow boot made from sealskin or reindeer skin and derived from the word *muklok*, meaning large seal

Pemmican a form of dried, pulverized meat mixed with fat and used by Native peoples as a concentrated food source

Pharology the science of lighthouses and signal lights

Pinniped a group of aquatic carnivorous animals, such as seals and walruses, having flippered feet

Red serge the trademark scarlet tunic worn by officers of the Royal Canadian Mounted Police; now the official dress uniform of the RCMP

Sam Brown Belt an officer's belt with a diagonal strap across the right shoulder that disperses the weight of a gun or saber. A Sam Brown belt is an important part of Fraser's red serge uniform.

Sea otter (*Enhydra lutris*) a large marine otter that floats about in fronds of kelp in Northern Pacific regions. Such animals have been known to be used as weapons by intoxicated individuals in the North.

Semaphore a means of communicating by positioning one's arms in certain ways to represent the letters of the alphabet; useful in instances where cellular phones and other means of communication are impossible

Shellac a preparation derived from the lac bug of India and used as a wood preservative for dock pilings; also employed by criminals to preserve their dead victims

Stop! the instruction from the human operator of a dogsled to running dogs up front to halt. The command has no effect, and novice sledders will soon learn to use a sled brake (*also see* Gee, Haw *and* Mush).

Ulu a crescent-shaped knife used by Native peoples of the North to cut meat, particularly in the preparation of seal blubber

Top 10 Episodes

"Chicago Holiday (I and II)"
Fraser finds out what the North American teen scene is all about when he is enlisted as the chaperone for the daughter of a Canadian diplomat. What seems like an easy assignment turns into a wild ride for the Mountie who gets to experience first-hand the shenanigans of a precocious sixteen-year-old. Under Fraser's charge, Christina Nichols introduces the Mountie to the vagaries of The House of Detention, an after-hours S&M bar, and the trials and tribulations associated with wanting to be an adult. While Christina tries to elude Fraser she unknowingly acquires something that a killer pursued by Ray and the Chicago Police Department wants. In the hijinks that follow, Fraser ends up on a white-knuckle toboggan ride down an escalator, shimmying around on the top of a speeding taxi, and plummeting down a garbage chute.

Episode Rundown

Due South Web Sites

The World Wide Web is ablaze with chat areas, sites and fan fiction of interest to fans and fanatics alike. Follow these links to discover *Due South* on line.

The OFFICIAL *Due South* Page (Canada)
www.duesouth.com

AC's *Due South* Page (USA)
www.cs.virginia.edu/~acc2a/ds/ds.html

Belinda's *Due South* Page (Australia)
www.ozemail.com.au/~blinda/belsds.htm

Bianca's *Due South* Page (Dutch)
www1.tip.nl/users/t799913

Bobby T's *Due South* Page (USA)
www.bobbyt.com/duesouth.html

Ed Carp's *Due South* Pages (USA)
dal1820.computek.net (contains links to DS sites)
wats-ts4-12.ppp.iadfw.net/pub/DueSouth
(contains .WAV files and various GIF and JPG files)

Louise Cause's *Due South* Page (Australia)
www.world.net/~gcause/dues.html

Nicola Gale's *Due South* Page (UK)
members.tripod.com/~Benton/index-1.html

Sharon Gillson's *Due South* Page (USA)
www.geocities.com/Hollywood/6805/dsmenu.htm

Nicola Heiser's *Due South* Page: (Australia)
www.uq.edu.au/~zznheise/DSOUTH.HTM

Nadine Killiard's *Due South* Page: (UK)
www.geocities.com/TelevisionCity/1415

Gabrielle LaFleur's *Due South* Page: (Canada)
www.navi.net/~gabrielle/DueSouth.html

LJC's *Due South* Page (USA)
www.geocities.com/~uisgejack/dsouth

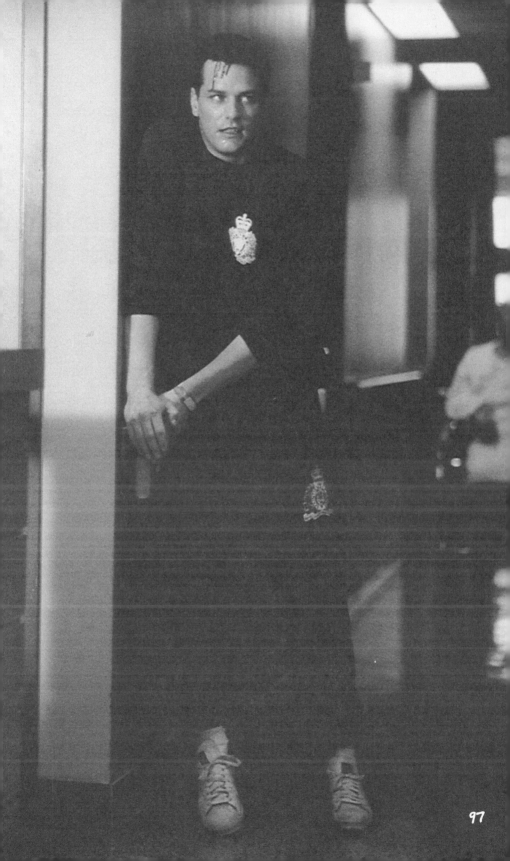

Due South Web Sites

Ken Lyons' *Due South* Down Under Page (Australia)
www.ozemail.com.au/~klyons/dsouth/ds_au.html

Brian & Sandy MacGowan's *Due South* Page (Canada)
www.interlog.com/~macgowan/DueSouth.html

Marie's *Due South* Page (Denmark)
www.geocities.com/area51/9034/DS.html

Marty's *Due South* Page
ds.dial.pipex.com/marty/dues.htm

Caroline Mockett's *Due South* Page (UK)
www.netlink.co.uk/users/mockett/duesouth.html

Pacific's *Due South* Page (UK)
www.pacificp.demon.co.uk/ds.htm

Helen Paridis' *Due South* Page (Australia)
www.ozemail.com.au/~pairidis/dueSOUTH/INDEX.html

Paula Piatt's *Due South* Page (USA)
www.cyber-quest.com/home/piatt/ds.html

PJ's *Due South* Page (UK)
www.users.zetnet.co.uk/brock/dspage.htm

William Rydbom's *Due South* Page (USA)
fly.hiwaay.net/~warydbom/duesouth.htm

Alexander Scheck's *Due South* Page (Austria)
www.geocities.com/SouthBeach/5491/dsindex.html

Sheila's *Due South* Page (USA)
www.geocities.com/Hollywood/4928/dsouth.html

Lorene Turner's *Due South* Page (Canada)
duke.usask.ca/~turner/duesouth.html

Elaine Walker's *Due South* Page
www.geocities.com/Hollywood/Set/4869/index.html

Deb Walsh's *Due South* Page (USA)
members.aol.com/debwalsh/ds.html

Related Sites

Melissa Banczak's RCW 139 Page
www.thequest.net/tceb/rcw139.htm

Detective Armani Fan Club (UK)
www.geocities.com/TelevisionCity/3046

Nicole Parrot's RCW Photo Page (Canada)
www.odyssee.net/~nparrot

Paul Gross photo page
www.geocities.com/Hollywood/Set/3234/paul2.htm

More Paul Gross photos and quotes from *Due South*
www3.fast.co.za/~tmar/welcome.html

RCW 139 - 1996 (USA)
fly.HiWAAY.net/~warydbom/duesouth/rcw139/main.htm
(official site for the fan-run 1996 *Due South* convention)

RCW 139 - 1997 (USA)
fly.HiWAAY.net/~warydbom/rcw1997
(official site for the fan-run 1997 *Due South* convention)

TCEB (Canada)
www.thequest.net/TCEB
(devoted to actor Tony Craig [Det. Jack Huey in *Due South*])

Various Paul Gross Movies (USA)
www.mcs.net/~feden/pgmovies.html

Alliance Television
www.alliance.ca

Nettwerk Records
www.nettwerk.com

Royal Canadian Mounted Police
www.rcmp-grc.gc.ca (official)
www.cs.uregina.ca/~mcintyre/rcmp.museum/rcmp.html (unofficial)

SYMPATICO
www1.sympatico.ca/Features/TV/duesouth.html

The gruesome threesome troll Chinatown for clues and leads. ("Chinatown")

Santa Claus is coming downtown: Santa Claus becomes a suspect in a bank robbery as Fraser and Ray step in to save Christmas. ("The Gift of the Wheelman")

Scrapbook

Top 10 Episodes

"Mountie on the Bounty (Parts 1 and 2)"

It's time to practice maritime law as Fraser and Stanley take to the high seas to fight crime and corruption on open water. Well, sort of: In fact, the two find themselves aboard a sinking Great Lakes freighter after following a lead muttered in the last, dying gasps of Billy Butler, a sailor who expires after a knife is plunged in his back. Butler's dying words "treasure chest" suggest to the two investigators that it's not all fish sticks, tartar sauce, and merrymaking in this sailor's life. And how is a bar of gold in the bottom of the dead sailor's sea chest related to rumors of ghost ships on the Great Lakes? And why is Billy Butler reported as missing on the list of freighter that sank a year ago?

Questions turn to adventure when Fraser and Kowalski take jobs as deck hands on a freighter to find out what's really going on. When Kowalski is hand-cuffed below decks by Vic Hester, another crew member on board, and the freighter begins to sink after being fired on by a "ghost ship," Fraser comes to the rescue just in time to release the detective from the handcuffs, saving him from drowning as the ship fills with water.

Fraser and Kowalski manage to dial in the ship's coordinates just before Kowalski's cell phone goes dead. Between the time Insp. Thatcher and Lt. Welsh are trying to locate their missing officers and figure out what the numbers received from Kowlaski's cell phone mean, the gold bar found in Billy Butler's sea chest is traced to a notorious heist of the Chicago Federal Reserve Bank.

Fraser and Kowalski meanwhile get aboard the ghost ship that sank the freighter they were on and discover that it is in fact a salvage ship for the gold that disappeared in the notorious bank heist when the escape plane carrying the gold crashed in the lake. But more important, in some ways, the salvage ship is carrying toxic chemicals that could poison the environment. Thatcher figures out the numbers from Kowalski's phone are coordinates, and with the help of an eccentric Mountie named Sgt. Sam and a replica of the HMS Bounty, they swoop in for a swashbuckling rescue.

Acronyms Frequently Used by *Due South* Web Heads

ATQH ...."All the Queen's Horses" episode

BDTH ...."Burning Down the House" episode

BH ...."Bounty Hunter" episode

BTW ....By The Way

CBC ....Canadian Broadcasting Corporation

CTV..................Canadian Television Network

DM ....David Marciano

DMEB..................David Marciano Estrogen Brigade

DS..................*Due South*

DSAWKI ....*Due South* As We Know It

DSLWS ....*Due South* List Withdrawal Syndrome: symptoms of anxiety, etc., when a list member is denied access to the DSOUTH-L for a prolonged period of time

DSWS ....*Due South* Withdrawal Syndrome: symptoms of depression, anxiety, etc. that occur when Due South is pre-empted

DueSies ....favorite lines of dialogue, quotes, etc.

DueSers ....*Due South* fans

GRC ....Gendarmerie royale du Canada: RCMP in French

ICBD.................."I Coulda Been a Defendant" episode

IMO ....In My Opinion

IMHO ....In My Humble Opinion

JIB ...."Juliet is Bleeding" episode

LLDS..................Long Live *Due South*

LOL..................Laughed Out Loud

M&S.................."Mountie and Soul" episode

No60..................*North of 60*

OFC ....Our Favorite Cop

OFCC ....Our Favorite Chicago Cop

OFDM..................Our Favorite Dead Mountie: Fraser's father, Sgt. Robert Fraser

OFFCWS ....Our Favorite Female Cop Withdrawal Syndrome (Elaine)

OFM ....Our Favorite Mountie

OFRLM ....Our Favorite Real Life Mountie: Darrin Ramey, list member

OFRLMB................OFRLM's new baby, named Benton!

OFRLMW ....Our Favorite Real Life Mountie's Wife (Carol)

OFSDC ....Our Favorite Story Department Coordinator (Scott Cooper)

OFW ....Our Favorite Wolf

OGM ...."One Good Man" episode

OOFM,OFOM ....Our Other Favorite Mountie: Buck Frobisher

OTOH ....On The Other Hand

PG ....Paul Gross

PGEB ....Paul Gross Estrogen Brigade

PH ....Paul Haggis, *Due South* creator and producer

RCMP ....Royal Canadian Mounted Police

ROTFL ....Rolled On The Floor Laughing

ROTFLOL ....Rolled On The Floor Laughing Out Loud

RURRTT ....Reverse Underground Railroad Tape Tour: sending *Due South*–
                        related tapes from Canada on a tour of US homes, for *Due
                        South*–starved US fans

SFC ....Strong Female Character(s)

SRK ....Stanley "Ray" Kowalski

SSS ....Second Season Syndrome

TDL ....The Dragon Lady: Fraser's boss at the consulate

TIICACBS ....The Idiots In Charge At CBS

TPTB ....The Powers That Be

VS ...."Victoria's Secret" episode

VV ....Victoria. The first V stands for whatever you think of the character.

WOS ....Worshippers of Scott (see OFSDC)

YKYBWTMDSW ....You Know You've Been Watching Too Much *Due South* When …

The National Anthem of Canada

O Canada!

Our home and native land!

True patriot love in all thy sons command.

With glowing hearts we see thee rise,

The True North strong and free!

From far and wide,

O Canada, we stand on guard for thee.

God keep our land glorious and free!

O Canada, we stand on guard for thee.

O Canada, we stand on guard for thee.

"God Save The Queen":

The Royal Anthem of Canada

God save our gracious Queen,

Long live our noble Queen,

God save the Queen!

Send her victorious,

Happy and Glorious,

Long to reign over us;

God save the Queen!

Thy choicest gifts in store

On her be pleased to pour;

Long may she reign;

May she defend our laws,

And ever give us cause

To sing with heart and voice,

God save the Queen!

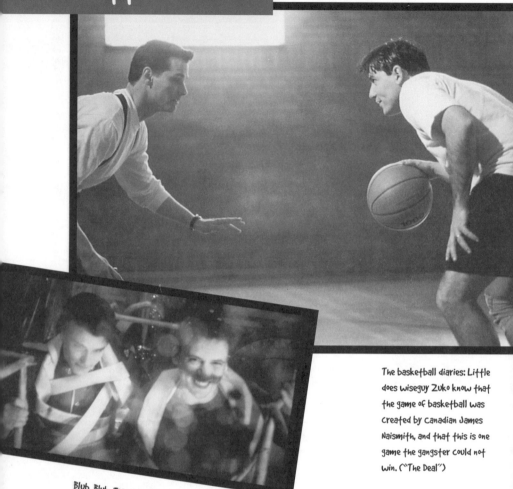

The basketball diaries: Little does wiseguy Zuko know that the game of basketball was created by Canadian James Naismith, and that this is one game the gangster could not win. ("The Deal")

Blub. Blub. Titanic mania, as appreciated by Fraser and Stanley. ("Mountie on the Bounty")

It's always a camping trip with Fraser. The two crime fighters in their old apartment. ("They Eat Horses, Don't They?")

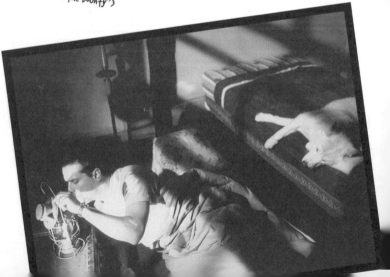

Dief's discerning palate at work. ("We Are the Eggmen")

Step right up folks and see the bearded lady, er Mountie ... Art for art's sake. Ms. Fraser conducts an art class. ("Some Like it Red Hot")

Sushi, anyone? The goldfish get saved in the fire at Ray's house. ("Burning Down the House")

credits

Acknowledgments

The editors acknowledge the participation of the following people in the preparation of this book: Eileen Morin (creative consulting), Robert I. Roll, C.F.P. (Montreal), Douglas Condon, C.A. (New York), Greg Stephens, Barrister and Solicitor (Toronto), Susan Renouf (Key Porter Books Ltd.), Mary Ann McCutcheon (Key Porter Books Ltd.), Derek Weiler (Key Porter Books Ltd.), Peter Maher (Maher Design), and Carmite Sadeh (Alliance Communications).

Produced by Michael Mouland expressly for Key Porter Books Ltd., Toronto.

www.interlog.com/~publish
P.O. Box 424
Station C
Toronto, ON
CANADA M6J 3P5